Get Your
Coventry Romances
Home Subscription NOW

And Get These
4 Best-Selling Novels
FREE:

LACEY
by Claudette Williams

THE ROMANTIC WIDOW
by Mollie Chappell

HELENE
by Leonora Blythe

THE HEARTBREAK TRIANGLE
by Nora Hampton

A Home Subscription! It's the easiest and most convenient way to get every one of the exciting Coventry Romance Novels! . . .And you get 4 of them FREE!

You pay nothing extra for this convenience: there are no additional charges. . .you don't even pay for postage! Fill out and send us the handy coupon now, and we'll send you 4 exciting Coventry Romance novels absolutely FREE!

SEND NO MONEY, GET THESE
FOUR BOOKS FREE!

C0482

MAIL THIS COUPON TODAY TO:
COVENTRY HOME SUBSCRIPTION SERVICE 6 COMMERCIAL STREET HICKSVILLE, NEW YORK 11801

YES, please start a Coventry Romance Home Subscription in my name, and send me FREE and without obligation to buy, my 4 Coventry Romances. If you do not hear from me after I have examined my 4 FREE books, please send me the 6 new Coventry Romances each month as soon as they come off the presses. I understand that I will be billed only $9.00 for all 6 books. There are no shipping and handling nor any other hidden charges. There is no minimum number of monthly purchases that I have to make. In fact, I can cancel my subscription at any time. The first 4 FREE books are mine to keep as a gift, even if I do not buy any additional books.

For added convenience, your monthly subscription may be charged automatically to your credit card.

☐ Master Charge   ☐ Visa
42101   **42101**

Credit Card #_____

Expiration Date_____

Name_____
(Please Print)

Address_____

City _____State _____Zip _____

Signature_____

☐ Bill Me Direct Each Month **40105**
Publisher reserves the right to substitute alternate FREE books. Sales tax collected where required by law. Offer valid for new members only. Allow 3-4 weeks for delivery. Prices subject to change without notice.

French
Jade

by

Rebecca Danton

FAWCETT COVENTRY • NEW YORK

FRENCH JADE

Published by Fawcett Coventry Books, CBS Educational and
Professional Publishing, a division of CBS Inc.

Copyright © 1982 by Rebecca Danton

ISBN: 0-449-50278-3

Printed in the United States of America

First Fawcett Coventry printing: April 1982

10   9   8   7   6   5   4   3   2   1

French
Jade

Chapter 1

MINERVA REDMOND sat in a corner, brooding. She wished she were anywhere in the world but here. She hated balls and detested games of whist.

She let her imagination riot for a time. She had been reading a book about the travels of an intrepid gentleman to South America, where Indians enjoyed the sport of shooting unwelcome visitors with poison-tipped arrows, then cutting off their heads.

Risky to travel there, yes, but it might be preferable to sitting on a flowered chintz sofa in a stuffy corner of a huge townhouse in London, waiting for partners to dance with one. And not wanting to dance with any gentleman any more than he wished to dance with one.

Oh, how miserable all this was! All the games one played in order to win a beau, and marry him, and be suitably set up in life. The only goal for a girl in Minerva's position in life was to marry, have children, raise them, and sit back complacently to watch the next generation play its games in turn.

When Oliver Seymour approached her, and held out his hand to her, she glared at him fiercely. He pretended to quail, his generous mouth quirked, he put his free hand to his heart.

"Come now, Minna, have I neglected you so, that you glare at me? You like to waltz, do you not? And you are old enough to do so, it is not your first season!"

She bit her lip to keep back angry words. She rose, in silence, and accepted his big hand to lead her back to the large open ballroom of the Lavery townhouse. How he could jeer and remind her it was her *third* London season, and she was neither married nor engaged!

"I do not see your brother Percy," he commented, as they took their positions on the shining parquet floor. He put his right hand firmly on her waist, and clasped the other about her slim right hand.

"No, he does not come to London just now. The estates require much of his time," she said primly.

"Yes. So do mine." He grimaced. "I found them in bad condition when I returned from the wars."

She relaxed a little. She did feel sorry for Oliver at times. He could be a terrible tease, but when she remembered what he had gone through, she felt quite weepy. He had been a spy for Wellington on the Peninsula, all through the terrible battles there. Then as though that were not enough, he had returned to the fray after recovering from a severe hip wound, to take part in the Battle of Waterloo, at which he had acquitted himself with such heroism that he had won several medals, which he firmly refused to wear. One could only silently admire such a man.

"I have not seen you in Kent," she said, a little more brightly. "We are quite near, Percy said."

"Yes, we are. I saw Percy around Christmas at Maidstone, but he had little time to pause and talk. When we all return to Kent, we must arrange little parties, eh?"

When he spoke so kindly, she could like him. He was

8

a wealthy man, but with no title, and he seemed to understand Percy and his problems with the estates.

"I would have thought he would have the matters well in hand. He inherited three years ago, I believe?"

"Yes, three years ago." Minerva said it dully, for Percival had inherited on the death of her beloved father. It had been so sudden, so shockingly unexpected—he had been there, big and bluff and helpful. Then he was gone, and all of them groping about blindly trying to think what to do without him.

Oliver squeezed her waist with his hand, and said, "Come now. This is a party, Minna! Chirk up. Has Percy settled on one of the pretty Misses Lavery?"

Percy was very fond of the second daughter, Denise Lavery, but Minna had no intention of telling Oliver so. Some things were private, after all.

"I would not know," she said, with a return of her prim manner. She straightened her shoulders in the ruffled white muslin, and glanced over to the lovely Denise in her favorite sapphire blue silk. Mr. Lavery was a silk merchant; it seemed all the girls always wore such lovely garments. Minna felt a flicker of envy, then forgot it. She could wear silks, she just did not choose to do so.

"Oh, prunes and prisms," said Oliver, with a laugh. "You must forget your books and learned papers while you are out for an evening, Minna! Learn to laugh and be gay. Men don't like a glum look, you know!"

"No," she said savagely, unable to stop herself. "Men like females who flirt with them, and let them kiss in corners, and act the fool!"

Oliver stared down at her, and she blushed hotly.

9

She had been thinking of her cousin Gabrielle, and let the words run away from her.

"You are quite right," he said soberly, but there was a twinkle in his dark gray eyes. His dark curly hair waved back from his broad bronzed forehead, and vaguely she admired his looks. He was tall, a little taller then her brother Percival. He limped a bit from his injury, but carried himself with grace, and danced well. But damn it, she thought, borrowing Percy's language, he could be such a devil of a plaguey man. "I am surprised you know about that, Minna! Surely not from your sober brother?"

"Percy is a good man, and a fine one, and the girl who marries him will be a lucky one!" Minna cried out, furious at his seeming scorn.

"Did I say otherwise? Come on, now, what's got into you? You're very hard to please, I must say," he said plaintively.

"I'm sorry," she said stiffly, and turned her head away so he could not see her face.

The waltz finished, she had scarcely noted how he carried her through it with grace and polish. "Will you have an ice?" he asked.

She was hot, more from his baiting than the dance. "I would like it, yes."

He bowed her into a corner near one of the older women, and went off to fetch it. The lady was Mrs. Lavery, brisk and practical—she had to be, with her four daughters and two sons, thought Minna.

"Are you enjoying yourself, Miss Redmond?" asked Mrs. Lavery kindly. She wore a dark purple silk, probably from her husband's warehouse.

"Yes, very much, thank you, ma'am. Your house is

always so cool and comfortable," added Minna, conscientiously. The Laverys entertained lavishly, always inviting all their children's friends as well as their own. "Such a lovely ballroom."

"Thank you, my dear. The girls arranged the flowers. Your mother looks delightful this evening, as always." Both of them looked toward where Mrs. Betsy Redmond talked and smiled in the center of a little group. Her mother wore black lace, she was still in mourning for her husband, dead these three years. But her face was calm and controlled, sweetly pleasant.

Oliver Seymour returned with three ices on a tray, and handed one to Mrs. Lavery with a smile. "Thank you, Mr. Seymour. May we look for your mother to come this spring?"

"If she can tear herself away from my sister and the children," he replied. "Eleanor's fourth has arrived, and Mother hovers with delight."

Mrs. Lavery looked at him shrewdly. "She probably has only one wish in the world to make herself completely happy," she said, significantly.

Oliver Seymour looked self-conscious. "Whatever do you mean, madam?"

"Your marriage, and heirs to inherit your beautiful property in Kent, sir, as you well know!" she said, with a laugh, and a tap of her fan on his arm. "Sterling Heights is a most beautiful place. You'll not leave it to your sister's children? She and her husband have their own place. The wars put you off long enough, sir!"

"You have guessed it, Mrs. Lavery," he said, with a sigh, and a comical grimace, while Minna stood eating her ice, with eyes cast down in some embarrassment. Why did older women choose the oddest occasions

11

to be familiar? "Mother tells me, I must find someone soon, or put myself on the shelf as a hopeless, crusty old bachelor!"

The two of them laughed, as though it was funny. Minna felt very odd, and cross. Why was it funny to be an old bachelor? When it was pathetic and sad to be an old maid? Life was not fair!

"Well, I would offer you one of my own fair daughters, but here is pretty little Miss Redmond," said Mrs. Lavery, trying to be kind. "You are in your third season, dear?"

Minna knew her cheeks were fiery red, and she felt so furious at Mrs. Lavery she could have screamed! "Yes, my third, Mrs. Lavery," she said. "And I really do not care! I have my books and my writing, and just last week one of my articles was published in the *Ladies' Gazette*—"

Oliver gave a guffaw. "Oh, come on now, Minna! Don't be a bluestocking," he said roughly. "You're not suited to that role!"

"I had an excellent governess!" She gasped at his rudeness. "She always encouraged me to develop my mind."

He looked down her, in what she thought was a very forward manner. "That isn't what a man looks for," he said.

Even Mrs. Lavery was somewhat shocked. "Mr. Seymour!" she rebuked, covering her mouth with her gloved hand. "Whatever would your dear mother say?"

"She would agree," he said. "She knows what's what! Well, if I have shocked you with my language, forgive me! But, Minna, don't be a fool, or you'll never catch
12

yourself a man!" And with this crass statement, he stalked off.

Mrs. Lavery was trying not to laugh, and that enraged Minna even further. "What a rude man," said Minna grimly.

"But he is right, my dear," sighed Mrs. Lavery. "I have encouraged my girls to learn how to sew, cook, manage a household, ride well, develop some nice hobbies. But after all, what a man does look for is pretty looks, nice, manners, and a good figure! What a world it is, to be sure."

"To be sure," echoed Minna, and left her hostess as the woman was distracted by a servant whispering about the refreshments.

She sat down in another corner, hoping she was hidden from the little throng of guests. Some went on dancing to a very good little orchestra in the shining ballroom. Others drifted to other rooms, where whist games, bridge, and even loo were being played. The Laverys believed in giving their guests what polite entertainment they wished.

Minna's thoughts had gone to Gabrielle Mably, her cousin. Oh, how Gabrielle would have reveled in this evening, and the coarse talk of Oliver Seymour! She would have agreed completely!

Minna had always been shy and quiet. Her brother Percy had been her best friend. Her father had understood her. Her mother had quietly encouraged her and supplied her with a fine governess, Miss Cratchford.

Then in 1811, Gabrielle Mably had come to stay with them, from France. Her parents had been killed in the Napoleonic Wars, and poor dear Gabrielle had nobody, said Mrs. Redmond, compassionately.

Gabrielle was everything that Minna was not. She was three years older, and a dozen years wiser about men and life. She was chic, even at her young age. She was smart, flirtatious.

Both girls had curly red hair, green eyes, slim rounded figures. Gabrielle was one inch taller, that was all the difference, as Betsy Redmond often said, in a puzzled way. But how different—

Minna had her hair in a long childish braid. Gabrielle had hers in little curls and ringlets that made men long to pull them—or kiss them. Minna had a childish face. Gabrielle had smooth, painted cheeks, long eyelashes, a knowing look, and men always wanted to pull her into corners of the dark garden and kiss her. Minna had found her on four different evenings, with four different men, as she told her mother in amazement.

Men flocked about Gabrielle like moths about candleflames. And how they loved to get burned! She had drawn men to her, laughed and teased them, flirted with them. And they never looked at all at Minna. They did not even see her. Minna had withdrawn deeper into corners, watching in awe and, yes, jealousy.

Gabrielle had remained with them for three years. The damage was done. While Minerva was in her most vulnerable teenage years, Gabrielle had been there, to outshine her, push her into corners, attract every man for miles around, make Minna all the more shy and retiring. Minna had not developed emotionally. At eighteen, she had come out in London, but she was hurt, stunted, as much by the teenage years with Gabrielle as by her father's death.

She had no confidence in her powers of attraction. Whenever she was with a man, she had thought of
14

Gabrielle, laughing, winking, teasing, flirting. She could not act like that, she had told herself. Everyone would laugh at her, as Gabrielle had laughed at her.

Her little successes had been in the schoolroom, with her writing of articles, her watercolors, which were very nice. She could play the piano nicely, and entertain her father's guests—when Gabrielle was out. Her family had modest wealth, she could dress as she liked. But muslin gowns of white and pale blue suited her, she had told her mother. She could not wear the bold low-cut dresses of silk and lace, like Gabrielle. She was not that kind, she knew it. Everybody would laugh.

Oliver Seymour glanced at little Minna in the corner, and shook his head. He led out Denise Lavery and said briskly, "What a pleasant party, Miss Lavery! Everyone is always welcome in your house, and you make us feel such warmth of polite pleasure."

She smiled up at him, and he felt a little jolt. She was a very pretty girl, just nineteen, in her second season. She was pretty, practical as well, much like her good mother. A man could do worse than court Denise Lavery. Her father was newly rich, a merchant of silks, and would settle a good dowry on each of his daughters.

Denise was the second of four girls. There was Mary, at twenty-one, more plain but a good-hearted girl. There was Amelia, seventeen, a bit shy, but lovely. And then little Jane, at fifteen, just beginning to bloom.

He wondered how serious Percival Redmond was about Denise. He would not want to cut out that nice lad. He had problems enough. He thought of the last time he had seen Percy, the worried lines about his green eyes. The boy worked hard, he had had little time to learn the estate work from his father. He must see

15

to him when he returned to Kent, perhaps he could help him.

"It is most kind of you to say so, Mr. Seymour. Do you remain long in London?"

He must remain long enough this time to find himself a bride, he thought, even as he spoke idle pleasantries to Denise Lavery. His mother had had a long talk with him. Oliver was now thirty-two, he had his estates in hand, he needed sons and heirs. He really must set down to the task of finding a suitable mistress for Sterling Heights. The Seymours had had the estates for three hundred years, it would not do to leave them to his sister and her sons. Not unless he must.

And he was young and vigorous, he was fed up with wars and death and violence. He wanted to marry, to dally with a pretty girl, kiss her senseless! His desires rose up in him, he was ready for the next part of his life. He wanted to become a lover, a husband, a father, even. Yes, he had enjoyed the weeks with his sister and her little family. To have a little boy cling to his leg and beg for a ride on his black stallion, to set a pretty little girl on his knee and sing her a naughty war song, to feel the helpless little bundle of a baby in his arms— Yes, he was quite ready for marriage.

But to what girl? He had no liking for some money-hungry female, brazen and ready to lead him a merry dance. He wanted some nice young girl, with laughing lips and innocent eyes, a virgin bride that was his to teach the pleasant lessons of marriage. Yes, he wanted a lively and lovely young bride. But who? He looked with speculative eyes about the merry company. This was why he was here in London this season. He wanted to return home an engaged man, if not married.

16

He changed partners, this time choosing young Astrid Faversham. The girl was tall, eighteen, in her first season. He took her on his arm, and escorted her into the set of eight persons.

He did not know her well; they had met only a couple of weeks ago. He asked her several questions, and found her quite pretty, though her silver blond hair looked a bit touched up, and her eyes were cold and gray as an icy stream. Her ice-blue gown showed a fine figure, though. Perhaps he was wrong about her. Blondes sometimes did seem cold.

"You have been in London for some time?"

"Only since March, sir. My father determined it was time I came out."

"You are from the north of England, by your accent?"

"Yes, sir. Do you like my accent?"

"Charming," he said automatically, though he found it rather Scottish. She smiled, showing her pretty, small teeth, like that of a cat.

He glanced about. Minerva Redmond was sitting in a corner again. In her white frilly muslin dress, she looked a dowd, he thought disapprovingly. And why did she tie up her long, curly red hair like that? She looked ten years older than her age.

A mischievous impulse overtook him. The girl needed stirring up. If she could only see herself as a man did! He steered Astrid over in that direction, and saw Minerva shrink back further behind a flowered curtain.

"Have you met Miss Minerva Redmond, Miss Faversham?" he asked, a little loudly.

"Sir? Oh, yes, I believe so. Does she not have hair of a disagreeable red shade? And some pretensions of intellect?"

"The very one," said Oliver, with intent. "She could be quite pretty, if she but dressed herself better, and found a finer hairdresser! But she will wear dowdy clothes! I find her dull, dowdy, and dour."

Astrid gasped at such frankness. She gazed up at Oliver with open pink mouth, like a kitten. She began to laugh. "Oh, sir, how too funny you are! Yes, indeed, she is that! Dull, dowdy, and dour!"

The set ended, and Astrid promptly repeated Oliver's remark to Mrs. Lavery. The good woman looked disapprovingly at the two of them. "Indeed, what a thing to say," she said coldly. "Miss Redmond is a fine lady, to my mind!"

Astrid went on to repeat the remark, uncaringly, to the next woman she met. Oliver was beginning to be very sorry he had said anything at all. Astrid was a very cat, he thought, and could have slapped her. But it was his own fault.

When the girl began to repeat the remark to still another gentleman, Oliver said brusquely, "That is enough, my girl! I should have said nothing. Let it go, I said!"

"But your remark describes her so well, and so cleverly!" cried Astrid, and her cold gray eyes glittered. "Dull, dowdy, and dour. You are a very poet!"

He gritted his teeth, and left her abruptly. He looked about for Minerva, resolved to apologize, or say something pleasant to her, to make up. But he did not find her.

Minna had heard it all too well. Incredulous, she had heard her recent escort declaim her qualities in such unflattering manner to that little cat, Astrid Faversham.

18

She told her mother, "I must go home, I will go! I shall not endure remaining with that—that cad!"

"He did not mean it, he was jesting," said Betsy Redmond. "Come, dear, do not take it to heart."

Tears glistened in Minerva's green eyes. "He is a beast, and I hate him! I'll pay him back one day, see if I don't!"

"Now, now, don't be childish. All right, I'll call our carriage, come along—don't cry, dear!"

"Cry! I'm blazing mad, I am, and I'll kick him in his wounded leg if I get a chance!"

Betsy Redmond sighed. "Sometimes I think none of you have grown up," she muttered, and went to the hall to find their coachman.

In the hallway, Mrs. Lavery stopped them for a moment. "Oh, dear, I am so sorry, Mrs. Redmond. I know Mr. Seymour meant nothing by the remark—oh, dear—"

"He is a crude, vulgar slow-top, and he means nothing to me," said Minerva with dignity, pulling her shawl about her. "Only a fool would take notice of what he says!"

"Of course, dear," said Mrs. Lavery, patting her shoulder. "Do come back to tea, Mrs. Redmond. Perhaps on Thursday?"

They went home in silence. Mrs. Redmond was exhausted. Getting Minerva married off was much more of a problem than she had ever dreamed it would be. Would she have such problems with Percival? If so, she would regret all the more the death of her dearest husband. He had always been such a comfort to her, such a stalwart staff.

Minna was humiliated, huddled there in her shawl

against the cold April wind. She hated all men, but most especially Oliver Seymour. And she would have vengeance on him! One day, she would have him groveling at her feet.

She did not know how she would manage it, but manage it she would! Oliver Seymour should crouch at her feet, and beg for pardon! And she would kick him, she would!

Chapter 2

JESSIE CAME into the darkened bedroom, snapped open the draperies, and cried out cheerfully, "Good morning, Miss Minerva!"

Minerva lifted her head from the lace-trimmed pillows and glared. "I have not slept a wink all the night!"

Jessie put her hands on her stout hips and surveyed her mistress shrewdly. "Too many late nights, I'll warrant. Will you wear a white muslin today, miss?"

"No," snapped Minerva. She pulled herself upright, and sat against the pillows to drink her tea. "No. Jessie—you looked after my cousin Gabrielle while she was here. Did she not leave some garments behind her, in the guestroom wardrobe?"

The older Irish maid looked puzzled, but nodded. "Indeed, she did. Said the gowns were too small for her, or some such. And there's a couple hats with flowers, and some worn shoes."

"Bring them here, Jessie," said Minna, and drank her tea while the maid shrugged and went to fetch the garments.

It took two maids to bring the garments into Minerva's large room. The gowns were spread across chairs, the hats laid on tables, the shoes set about. And there was a beaded handbag, some veiling, and a box of half-used cosmetics, rouge and powder and black stuff Minna remembered Gabrielle using on her eyes.

"Will you be wearing them to a masquerade, miss?" asked Jessie, with the familiarity of long service. She held up a green jade silk gown, with low-cut bosom and some bedraggled cream lace. She sniffed. "Indeed, your cousin showed no shame when she wore this one!"

"Let me see it." Minna hopped out of bed, and held the gown up against herself. The length was right, Gabrielle usually wore her gowns a bit short, to show her slim shapely ankles.

"Shameless," muttered Jessie, and went to pour hot water in the tub in the old-fashioned bathroom next to Minna's bedroom.

Minna bathed, and returned to her room. She put on one of the abandoned petticoats, and some fine lace stockings, then tried on the high-heeled green slippers. She tottered about the room, as Jessie watched her curiously.

Then she had Jessie help her on with the green silk. It was low cut, but not badly. The bosom was rounded, and showed the tops of Minna's creamy breasts. And I do have a nice shape, she thought to herself, eyeing herself in the tall mirror beside her dresser.

"Now, what would you be up to, miss?" asked Jessie, her suspicions growing.

"You did Gabrielle's hair for her, Jessie. Fix my hair like hers, all curls and wisps."

To her surprise, Jessie made no protest. She set to with a will and a brush, and stroked the curly hair, and whipped it up with a comb, until Minna's hair looked quite unlike its usual sleek self. There were long sausage curls beside her creamy white throat, wisps of curls at her forehead and beside her small ears, and

22

her face looked small and demure in the billowing masses of red-gold curls.

She looked like Gabrielle.

Minna picked up the rouge pot, and the little camel's hair brush, and began to dab, cautiously, then more daringly. Then she added some white powder on her nose and chin and forehead. Jessie watched alertly, then added a little black to her reddish gold eyelashes, and gradually Minna's face altered. She looked—daring! Older! Fashionable! Flirtatious!

It was amazing what a little makeup would do, thought Minna, studying herself critically.

"And now what, miss?" asked Jessie.

"I'll show Mother," said Minna, and got up to go downstairs.

"You look grown up," said Jessie, amazed. "You won't do wrong to look a bit more flashy, miss!"

Flashy! Well, maybe that was what she wanted, thought Minna, teetering cautiously down the stairs on the high-heeled green silk shoes. The footman stared at her, and hastened to open the doors to the drawing room.

Mrs. Betsy Redmond was seated on the rose silk sofa, attired in a fine gray striped silk and waiting for any guests who might come that morning. She glanced up from her small book of poetry which she often read, and gazed at Minerva. Then astounded, she rose, and cried, "Why—Gabrielle! What a pleasant surprise!"

Minerva went right into the outstretched arms, and cooed on impulse, *"Chère Tante* Betsy! How delicious to see you! It has been such a long-g-g time since we meet, yes?"

To her pleased ears, she sounded just like Gabrielle, with French accent and gushing manner.

Mrs. Redmond hugged her, kissed her cheek cautiously, with care for the makeup. "You did not write? But you must remain here, my dear—how did you come, do you have an escort?"

"No, no, I come by myself, I long-g-g to see my dearest *tante,* I cannot wait for an escort—"

Mrs. Redmond drew back, frowned slightly and searched the face of Minna. Minna could not restrain a wicked grin. "Gabrielle—" Her mother hesitated. Then she cried, "No, no, it is not—it is—Minna, what have you done?"

Minna laughed with pleasure. "I fooled you! My own mother! I fooled you! Then I can fool society and that awful Oliver Seymour. I shall do it!"

Her mother took her in, from the curly hair and flowered hat, down the jade green gown, to the slightly worn shoes, and shook her head. "Oh, my dear Minna." She sighed. "What shall you do? What mischief is this?"

"I have decided to masquerade as Gabrielle!"

"No!"

"Yes, I shall," said Minna, with unusual passion. "I am tired of being Minerva, so sensible and bluestocking, so dull and dowdy and dour! I shall shock London to its boots! And shake up that self-satisfied Mr. Seymour! I am going to take London by storm!"

Mrs. Redmond surveyed her daughter in silence for a time. Then she sank down onto the sofa again, and patted the seat beside her. "Sit down, darling. Let us talk," she said gravely. "I know you were hurt last night. But Oliver is a good-hearted man, he will apologize for his impulsive words—"

24

"On his knees!" said Minna. "One day, he will go down on his knees and apologize to me! I won't be satisfied until he does! Meantime, I shall fool and mock him, until he doesn't know if he is on his head or his heels!"

"And how do you plan to do that?" asked Betsy Redmond, with gentle patience. "By seeing him once as Gabrielle? It is difficult to keep up a masquerade, as you may not know—"

"I can keep it up for a week or so, that is enough," Minna persisted stubbornly. She tossed her head, then found that dangerous, with her thick mass of curls and the flowered hat perched precariously on the top of the curls. She pushed the hat back into place. "I can mock Gabrielle's accent, and ape her manners, I watched her enough. I am so happee to see you today, *madame!* It has been the leetle while since we met each other, no? How sweet you look today, *chérie!*" And she patted her mother's hand impishly.

Mrs. Redmond had to laugh, and shake her head. "It does sound like Gabrielle, with her ways," she had to admit. "But it is different with a man, you know. She was very—flirtatious, and gay. And she was not averse to being kissed—Minna, you would hate it!"

Minna started to toss her head again, then clutched the hat with both hands, and stuck the hat pin in more firmly. "I shall do it," she said recklessly. "I don't care— I can do it, and I shall for a time. Just wait and see—"

"But what about—Minerva? You cannot be both!"

Minna felt a bit startled. "Let me see— She can be sick! Yes, Minerva has a fever, and has to stay abed! Gabrielle has come for a visit, and you shall show her
25

about London! Gabrielle shall fill Minerva's engagements, and go to parties without her dear sick cousin! That is it."

Her mother looked troubled. "My dear, I fear you will get into trouble," she said, gently, her graying red hair pressed back by her shaking hand. "Oh, dear, I don't want to discourage you, my dear. But I have not seen you so—so upset and passionate for a time! I fear you will be reckless, and lead on some young man—and then not know what to do about it. Your cousin was very—experienced, you see."

"Well, it is about time I got some experience, then," said Minna furiously, her eyes snapping. "She was but sixteen when she came, and she was—was always kissing young men in the bushes. So shall I, then!"

"Good heavens," muttered Mrs. Redmond. The footman opened the door, and announced guests sonorously.

"Mrs. Redmond, I have the honor to present—Mrs. Smythe-Jones, Mrs. Peeples, Miss Peeples, Miss Jensen—"

The four ladies swept in, some of Mrs. Redmond's dearest friends. The two women rose automatically. The curious looks swept over the strange lady at once, the woman in the smart French gown and huge, flowered hat.

"Good afternoon, dearest Mrs. Redmond. You have a guest?"

Minerva sensed her mother's reluctance, and swept some words in first. "I am her niece from France," she said sunnily. "May I introduce myself—Madame Gabrielle Mably Dubois—"

The footman's jaw dropped down. Minna gave him

26

a hard look. Mrs. Redmond hastily directed him to bring tea, and he bowed and left them.

The ladies were all introduced, and openly admired her. "What a charming niece—Madame Dubois? Your husband is with you? Oh, a widow—and so young and beautiful— Ah, the wars, so sad—you had a difficult time?"

Minna quite enjoyed herself. She had read all of Gabrielle's gossipy letters, and could supply all information easily. "Yes, my dearest Gaspar died more than a year ago, the war was hard on him—the estate? Inherited by my stepson."

Said stepson had at once swept Gabrielle out of the house and land, and back to Paris, where she lived in a converted mansion on one floor, as she lamented. But Minna did not say that. She left the impression of vast estates, wealth, a devoted stepson—some grief over the death of the elderly husband. She peppered her speech with a few Gabrielle-isms of speech, some bit of accent, not too much. After all, the girl had learned to speak English quite well. And Minna knew French as well as German. She carried it off beautifully. Her mother watched her keenly, ready to jump in if Minna faltered, but Minna did not falter.

Minna felt as though she were in a Christmas pantomime, playing not Little Bo-Peep, her usual role, but a beautiful fairy godmother, or glamorous Cinderella ready to go off to the ball! She quite enjoyed her new role. She spoke, she laughed, she glittered, she held the floor, she gossiped, she was charming to them all.

Never had she done this before. Her part had always been to be shyly welcoming, assisting her mother in entertaining, silently pouring tea, and handing around

27

cakes. Today, she let the footman hand things about, while her hands waved in the air, à la Gabrielle, and she dramatically told them all about the wars in France, her dear departed Gaspar, the time the soldiers came into the château and were quartered there for two months, and drank all the wine.

"And my most dears," she said, waving her hands, "how they have parties every night, and makes the trouble! And of course, they all weesh to dance with me and make my dear husband so jealous! The Captain, he says to me, if only I was not marry! And he drew his sword, and I thought he would make me a widow at once! What troubles! I had such a time, charming him to forget his deadly idea!"

Mrs. Redmond choked on her cake, and hid her face in her lace handkerchief.

By the time the ladies left, reluctantly, about twelve thirty, Minna was wildly triumphant. She had succeeded, she had fooled them all! Nobody among the ladies—all of whom had met Minerva Redmond time and again—had the least idea she was not the glamorous French cousin, Madame Dubois. And she had invitations for the next week for every day, to come to tea, to play cards, to drive in the park, to attend a ball—

"I am a success, Mother!" Minna gasped as the door finally closed on them. She danced around the room, tripped on the carpet edge, and clasped a chair to keep from falling over. "These dratted heels! But I will learn to walk on them!"

Betsy Redmond collapsed on the sofa, and laughed and laughed, until the tears came to her eyes. She wiped them on the lace handkerchief, which had done yeoman service these two hours. "Oh, my dear, I have never seen such a play! I was so vastly amused! I never thought my daughter had such acting ability! Oh, dear, I must laugh again!"

Minna sat on the edge of a chair, and scowled. "I did well, didn't I?" she demanded doubtfully. "They did not guess, did they? I am sure they did not, I vow it!"

"No, I don't think so. But, my dear, it is different, fooling several older women, and fooling a young man who knows you—such as Oliver Seymour!"

Minna's green eyes flashed fire. "He does not know me! He thinks I am dull, dowdy, and dour! He has no idea of what I am like inside! He likes blondes like that nasty cat, Astrid Faversham. Well, I shall show him there are other females in the world, and more entrancing also! Wait until I lead him on to try to kiss me and embrace me, and then push him away! Wait until he has to line up for my favors at a dance, and I turn from him to—to someone more attractive!"

Mrs. Redmond eyed her daughter very curiously indeed. She was silent for a time, while Minna tried to cool her heated cheeks with her fan, waving it furiously before her face. Gabrielle had left this fan also, a beautiful black Spanish lace fan, which she had held before her, and peered over the edge of, and flirted with for hours on end. Minna could remember her using this fan to bring every young man in the room to her feet! Well, she would do that also!

"Well," said her mother slowly. "Well, you are committed for this next week, to tea at Miss Jensen's, and cards at Mrs. Smythe-Jones's—and we also are going to Oliver Seymour's townhouse for a ball on Friday—

29

I don't suppose it would hurt anything if you play the part of Gabrielle for a few days."

"I mean to," said Minna firmly, though she quailed a bit at the thought of stepping outside the house in this outfit. "I am going to play my part very well, you'll see!"

Mrs. Redmond nodded her head, she looked almost—satisfied, thought her daughter. "Well—yes. All right. We shall do our best to help you, Jessie and I. I won-der—are there persons in London who would remem-ber Gabrielle?"

Minna frowned. That would be a problem. "I don't think there would be many in our circle. We were mostly in the country, in Kent, during the war."

"Um—there were some married couples she met—but I don't believe—I will think about it. The Laverys did not know her—Mr. Seymour was on the Penin-sula—of course, Percival knew her, and Miss Cratch-ford—but they are not in London now. Gabrielle was quite a flirt, and attracted much attention, however. There may be some who recall her."

"She was a conniving girl, and I shall be just like her," said Minna, decidedly. "I shall pay attention to married men, and single, dance with whomever I like—dress extremely—"

"What gowns did Gabrielle leave? Any besides this one?"

"There is a green ball gown—and a peach walking dress that was shocking with her hair—and mine," added Minna with satisfaction. "I remember Papa say-ing only a daring girl like Gabrielle would wear peach with red hair."

"Yet she always looked stunning—even your father

thought so, for all the trouble she caused," said Betsy Redmond with a sigh.

"And there is a blue gown, very low cut—a funny shade of blue that Gabrielle liked, almost green, that changes color in the light."

"Oh, I remember that one. I wonder why she left that."

"The hem is torn."

"Oh. Well, we must go over the gowns, and get them in condition to be worn. Shall you want more dresses than these, Minna? We could go out shopping," suggested her mother casually, as they went up the stairs.

Minna looked at her mother with an aroused suspicion. Her mother was taking this almost too well. Did she have some motives, other than to give Minna some pleasure in her revenge?

"I don't think so, Mother, there is no use spending money for the gowns, when Gabrielle left some."

"If you change your mind, we can see Miss Clothilde during the week; she complained we had not bought anything for ages."

Minna frowned. She had refused to buy anything new for the season. Her gowns would do just as well, she had said, while cherishing a fond desire for one ball gown that would make Mr. Seymour sit up and take notice! Perhaps she could—but no, she would not give him the satisfaction of even imagining he had caused her to purchase a new gown for him to see!

She and her mother and Jessie went over the gowns; she tried them on, to find they fit rather well. Jessie sat down with sewing box and thread, to mend some rents and rips and take in the waist of the peach dress.

They had luncheon, her mother placid, while Minna

felt in a very fever of excitement. By the end of the week, she resolved to have Oliver Seymour at her feet! And as for that cat Astrid Faversham, she would have to think of some very fit punishment for her!

But the main object of her fury was Oliver Seymour. Pretending to be such a good, kind friend, then making remarks behind her back like that. Oh, boiling in oil would be too good! No, she must bring him down to some low level.

She would make him burn with desire for her, just as Gabrielle would do, then jeer at him as she unmasked! How delightful that would be!

She would say to him that he was a stupid fool who could not see real gold for dross! He would be courting a girl in a mask, in a guise, who was not real, who mocked him silently. And all the time, he had scorned a girl in plain clothes, who was intelligent and honest and—and good! No, men preferred flirts, and she would show him to his face what kind of man he was!

He had no regard for a fine, plain girl who preferred intelligent conversations to dancing, who preferred good music to whist. He would prefer a flirt in a low-cut dress, to a girl who was modest and fine.

Well, Minna would masquerade as a French jade, a very model of a wicked French girl, and see him fall at her feet! And then—oh, sweet revenge, when she unmasked, and told him—

"Minna, I have asked you three times, will you have mint jelly with your lamb?" asked her mother impatiently. "Why are you moving your lips and waving your hand?"

"Just—rehearsing, mother," said Minna, and her green eyes glittered. "I am going to enjoy this week!"

"Well, I have informed the footmen and the butler, the maids and the cook about all this," said Mrs. Redmond. "Dear me, it will be a bother for us all—but if it makes you happy, so be it!"

Chapter 3

BY THE TIME Friday came, Minna was well-rehearsed in her part of Gabrielle. She could even walk rather well on the high French heels. She had attended a whist party, talked well about her experiences in the war, her darling deceased husband, and the condition of France today. She had gone out walking, out riding, out to tea, in the peach gown, the green gown, and a splendid black and white striped dress.

Now it was time to appear before Oliver Seymour and dazzle him! The blue gown that was iridescent and splendid had been refurbished, and had fresh white lace at the throat and sleeves, courtesy of Jessie's clever needle. Minna had practiced dancing in a pair of French-heeled blue slippers, had waved the black Spanish fan before the mirror, and muttered several lines of dialogue to use with Oliver.

"Now, don't go too far," warned her mother anxiously, seeing the dangerous glint in her daughter's green eyes. "Gabrielle was accustomed to men, and how to handle them. Do not let any man go too far!"

"*Chère Tante* Betsy," cooed Minna devilishly. "Do not be anxious for me! I am French, and I can handle any man who ever strutted!"

Betsy Redmond giggled, showing a flash of the youthful charm which had so captivated Arnold Redmond. "Dear me, Minna, you are a caution!"

Minna took this as a compliment. Usually she was called intelligent, and sober, and such a good girl!

She set off in the carriage with her mother, feeling almost feverish with anticipation. The April night was cold, and she wore her mother's black velvet cloak over the blue, shimmering ball gown. It was so low cut, in spite of the white lace, when a man leaned over her in the dancing, he could see almost half her white rounded globes of breasts. But she would not care! She was the widow, Madame Gabrielle Dubois, stunning and desirable!

She had not seen Oliver Seymour this week. But she had practiced her manner and speech, her appearance, before her closest friends and those of her mother. None had guessed that she was really Minerva Redmond. She could easily fool Oliver as well, she knew it. And how delicious that would be!

The carriage rolled over the cobblestones and drew up in front of the splendid Seymour townhouse. It was ten times the size of the modest Redmond London house. White wings stretched across wide lawns, and torches blazed in the hands of footmen in white wigs who stood to light the guests inside. More lights flared in the long French windows in the house, set back in its surrounds of tall oaks and green, fragrant bushes.

Minna had been here a few times in the daylight, to tea or some musical event. But this was her first time for a ball in the grand Seymour mansion. She held her breath as she and her mother were greeted by a butler, and their cloaks removed.

They were shown into the first drawing room. More rooms echoed the grandeur of the first one, all opening to each other with wide sliding doors. Parquet floors

35

gleamed, precious Persian rugs silenced their steps as they moved to the reception line where Oliver stood.

How grand and formal he looked this evening! His slim height was set off by a green and gold outfit. His black curly hair was dressed à la Byron, his gray eyes gleamed as he saw Minerva approaching. His surprise showed as he looked from her to Mrs. Redmond and back again. Did he know her?

Mrs. Redmond said smoothly, though the lie must be choking in her throat, "Permit me to introduce to you my niece, Madame Gabrielle Mably Dubois, newly arrived from Paris. She stayed with us for a time during the late wars, and has just come to pay us a visit. My dear, this is Mr. Oliver Seymour."

Minerva curtseyed to him, deeply, permitting herself to bow in a manner that would show her bosom. She came erect, and caught a flare of interest and even desire in the gray eyes as he took her hand and raised it to his lips.

"Madame—Dubois? How pleasant to welcome you to my home. And your husband is not with you?"

Minerva put her handkerchief to her lips briefly, let her eyelids droop sadly. "My dear Gaspar, dead this year, I miss him so much! But life must go on, *n'est-ce pas?*"

"Oh, yes—yes—" He seemed in a daze. She snapped open the black fan, and gazed demurely over it at him. "Ah—you will dance—later?" he asked.

"I should adore it! But you will forgive me if I stumble over your feet, eh? My poor dear husband—I was in mourning, as you will see— Do I say it right?" She turned anxiously to her mother, who was having trouble controlling her expression.

36

"Yes, of course, my dear," said Mrs. Redmond. "We must stroll on—there are others behind us," she murmured.

Minna caught her mother's eye. Mrs. Redmond was worried that Minna would go too far. *"Mais, oui, Tante,"* she said demurely, and gave Oliver a little wink. "I see you—later, *monsieur?"*

"Oh, yes, definitely—" He swallowed on the words, and turned reluctantly to the next persons.

In the next room, Mrs. Redmond groaned. "Oh Minna—"

"We did not tell him Minna is ill," murmured "Gabrielle" pensively. "I think he forgot the poor girl!" Another score against him!

The rooms were very grand. They strolled about, took some refreshments in the way of small plates of pasties of meats and savories, had a drink of cool, refreshing chilled cordial. Oliver did entertain nicely, thought Minna critically, resolved to find fault, but finding nothing to fault.

The rooms were also decorated well—sparsely, nothing overwhelming, but in beautiful taste. Matching dark crimson draperies hung at the long French windows, with fresh white lace curtains just inside them. The ceilings were white stucco, with low-relief frescos of cupids and angels, and some little garlands of flowers. Some china cabinets of rosewood were set about, several holding precious and beautiful sets of porcelain, a blue set from China, another set in *famille rose,* another in an unusual pale green.

In the long room beyond the drawing rooms, dancing was in progress. Minna was immediately seized upon to make a set, and with her new animation was an

37

immediate favorite. She danced more wildly, she sparkled, she talked animatedly. All she had to remember was that she "knew" nobody and must be continually introduced to people she had known for years!

It was like being in a play, and she enjoyed herself very much. Nobody thought of her as shy, retiring, bluestocking Minna, nobody asked her about literature or the arts, all treated her as a fascinating French woman!

Within half an hour, Oliver Seymour claimed her as his partner. He had rushed through the lines of guests, and left a friend to greet any latecomers, she found. He clasped her hand, and asked the orchestra to play a waltz.

Minna followed his steps with ease—after all, she had often danced with him! But tonight, she felt unusually gay and free, and she laughed up at him as he whirled her about the huge ballroom. The candles glimmered in the window sconces, and were reflected in the full-length mirrors opposite. She caught sight of a woman with flowing red curls, a shimmering blue ball gown, a laughing face, and had to stare to make sure it was herself!

"When did you arrive from Paris?"

"About a week ago, *monsieur!*"

"Pray, call me Oliver! And I shall call you Gabrielle! Our families are very close friends, you know!"

So close he felt free to insult her! Minna's eyelids moved down on her smooth painted cheeks, she allowed herself a half smile. "Indeed. How kind you are. Englishmen are always so kind, I remember from my visit years ago!"

"And were all Englishmen—kind to you—then?"

38

His hand closed more tightly on hers, his arm crept more closely about her slim waist. She felt a little warm, he was holding her so tightly.

She allowed herself to look right up into his eyes. "Oh, *mais, oui,* so veree kind! All wanted to take me riding in the carriage, all wanted to show me their gardens—in the moonlight—and the stars, and to tell me the names of the pretty stars!"

The little smile curling her red lips seemed to fascinate him. "I'm sure that was very kind of the gentlemen," he said drily. "I would take you outside to show you the stars tonight, but in London one does not see them very well, and besides it is quite cold tonight!"

"Of course, I understand completely! And besides, you are the host, and cannot leave your guests!"

She did not know from where she had the nerve to talk to him like this! She had never done so before, she had never glanced upward and then half-closed her eyes, and fluttered her long lashes, which Jessie had covered with black paste. She had never allowed her clear voice to go husky with feeling, and to tease a man with subtle meanings.

He gave her up reluctantly to another man, danced with one of the older ladies, and returned swiftly to her side as the music changed to a polonaise. They swept through it, she thanking fortune that Percival had been so patient in teaching her all the popular dances of England and Europe. He enjoyed dancing, poor Percival, now stuck down in the country, working with cattle and pigs.

At the end of the lively Polish march, she was quite out of breath, and fanned herself vigorously with Gabrielle's Spanish fan. Oliver took it from her, managing to clasp her fingers briefly as he did so. "Permit me," he said, and fanned her so that her cheeks were cooler and her hair blew about her face. "What glorious hair you have, it is like sunlight!"

"Thank you, *monsieur*. How kind you are!"

"You have heard it all before," he said, a little roughly, his gray eyes unable to stay away from her face, her throat, her rounded white breasts. "Men must pay you compliments continually! You are so lovely, such a pretty figure, so rounded and feminine, such a lovely face, a perfect oval— And your eyes. My God, I could drown in that green ocean!"

Minna gulped, and tried to conceal her shock. No man had spoken so frankly to her before. He seemed to be eating her with his gaze. He had never acted so with her, he had always been laughing and teasing and big-brotherly with her.

"Are you warm? I'll take you to another room, it is cooler—" He put his hand under her elbow, and drew her with him, with determination. She was too flushed and flustered to protest, and in a few moments she found herself alone with him in a smaller room. Books lined the walls from floor to ceiling, except for the outer wall, which was French windows open to the night sky.

In the center of the room were several glass cases filled with green and white and rose objects. She looked at them curiously, and to distract him from staring at her, she asked, "What are these, *monsieur?*"

"These—ah, my jade collection. In the family for some generations," he said, and drew her to the nearest one. "Members of the family traveled much in the Orient, and even now I usually commission supercargoes on the trade vessels to find me the best jade when they go to China. These are some splendid pieces of white—called mutton fat, for their shiny appearance—"

She bent over the case to admire the pieces, beautifully carved into small animals, deer, and lions, and tigers, and some sea lions. "How very clever, and so pretty," she murmured.

Seeing her interest, he went on to tell her about other objects. "These green ones are the finest jade, green is much prized. In fact jade in China is more valued than gold or silver. It is considered a precious stone, from heaven, and many religious objects are carved from the largest, finest pieces. I was fortunate to obtain these fine goddesses—this is the Goddess of Mercy—"

They remained in the room for some fifteen minutes, while she genuinely admired the pieces he showed her. The rose jade gave her much pleasure, the color was so soft, and the objects usually of flowers and birds.

Another couple wandered into the library as they leaned over the case. The two gave Oliver and Minna curious looks. Minna was recalled to the impropriety of being here alone with her host, a male of very masculine manner.

"I am quite recovered and cool again," she said demurely. "Shall we return to your guests? I shall not be popular among the ladies if I detain you so long!" And she gave him a long, sideways look.

"Do you think I care about that?" he said in a low, passionate voice. "I could talk with you for hours, and not mind it!"

She was a little frightened by his intensity. How

would Gabrielle manage this? On impulse, Minna put her hand in his silk-clad arm, and felt the heat of him, and the beating of his heart under her hand. "Do come, Mr. Seymour," she cooed. "I do not wish my dear *tante* to be angry wiz me, for not minding the proprieties of British society!"

He drew a deep breath, and clasped her hand so close to his body that she could not free it. "Very well, we shall go, but only on the condition that I may have the next three dances!"

Three dances! That would be very rash! Everyone would talk! Minna managed to laugh a little, "But that is not fair to the other languishing ladies, Mr. Seymour!"

"I care not. And you must call me Oliver, I shall call you Gabrielle, whether you refuse me or no!"

They were strolling through the next drawing room, back toward the ballroom. Minna stammered a little as she felt him walk so close to her that his thigh brushed hers.

"Y-you g-go too fast, Mr. Seymour—I p-protest—"

He looked down at her as she gazed up at him, her eyes wide and green. "You are the most beautiful woman I have ever met," he said intensely. "I wish I had met you five years ago."

"Oh? Why?"

"Before you met—your husband," he said, in a low growl.

Minna tried to recover. "But—but, sir—I was but a green girl when I was here last—only nineteen when I left—"

"You must have been charming—so sweet and un-spoiled—"

42

Gabrielle, sweet and unspoiled? Minna gurgled out loud before she remembered herself. Gabrielle had been a flirt in her cradle, an experienced, cunning artificer when she staggered about in her first steps!

"Why do you laugh?" The deep voice demanded over her head.

"A private thought, *monsieur!*"

"I wish to know all your thoughts!"

"That would be most dangerous!"

He groaned. "Here we are, back among people. Oh, God, I wish to be alone with you again!"

She turned to him, and half raised her arms. "I thought you wished to dance, Oliver?" she drawled out his name wickedly, her eyes half shut. She put one hand on his arm, held out the other hand. He grabbed her into his arms, drew her to him, and began to dance, holding her so close she could feel the warmth of his body next to hers in the silky ball gown. He was staring down at her, she knew he could see the silky smooth white breasts that were rising and falling with her quickened breathing.

She had never been held so tightly. She thought of protesting primly—but Gabrielle would not! She would adore it, that French girl!

So Minna caught her breath and said bravely, "The music is so charming tonight!"

"You are so charming tonight."

"You are too—very gallant!"

"I am not gallant. I am overcome."

"Really," said Minna faintly. She felt rather overcome herself, warm and too close to him. How—how delicious it was to be held so in the dancing! She had never felt so before. But she rather enjoyed the fever

43

of his touch, the hard clasp of his big bronzed hand holding her hand so tightly.

"Why do you not wear a wedding ring?" he asked abruptly.

Oh. Why? Why? Minna's mind, rather faint and feverish, groped wildly for the answer. "I—I am so reminded—of my dear Gaspar—I thought I would leave it off—for a time," she managed to say, and peeped up at him to see if he would accept that as a good answer. Gray eyes burned down into hers.

"I think," he said deliberately, "that you are trying to forget him—and your marriage. It was not happy, was it?"

She gasped. "How c-can you s-say that—"

"You stammer when you are not sure of yourself," he said, quietly. "You are an odd mixture—sophistication and a rather sweet uncertainty—"

Uh-oh. She was letting Minerva show through Gabrielle's façade. Minna was silent through the rest of the dance, gathering her resources. At the end, she drew away from him firmly.

"You 'ave dance too much wiz me this evening, Monsieur Seymour, people will talk!" she scolded him brightly. "Now, you go off and dance—with zat one!" and she pointed to Astrid Faversham, who was gazing hungrily in Oliver's direction.

He grimaced, but went obediently to Astrid, and asked her to dance. Yet he kept glancing over her shoulder toward Minerva and amber-eyed Ross Harmsworth. Ross had been recently discharged from the military, and was telling Minerva all sorts of wild adventures he had had in the wars. She knew him; Minna had once

44

scolded him for making up his stories! But Gabrielle did not know that, of course!

Teddy Bailey danced with her next, and she was glad to dance with him. He was red-faced and stammered badly, but he was a kindly soul and good-hearted, and she liked him. She encouraged him brightly. "Yes, you did? How splendid. Is it very difficult to jump over ze fences with ze stallions?"

Over Teddy's sturdy shoulder she spied one of Denise's younger sisters, Amelia, looking anxious and forlorn. She sat on a straight chair in a corner, and had obviously dragged the chair from a set of several in one drawing room to its place by itself.

"Dear me, the poor child," said "Gabrielle," while Minna thought, She looks just like I always felt! "Do steer me in that direction, Teddy, if you will! I must speak to the child."

"Nice girl," said Teddy, blushing fire. He had an honest, open face, with a rough complexion, and turned bright red when embarrassed. "Always liked her. But she turned me down, said she can't dance well."

"Come back in ten minutes, will you, and be a dear?" said Minna confidingly, and pressed his arm and smiled up at him alluringly.

"Oh, yes, like a shot!" cried Teddy, and left her there in the corner, after dragging over a chair for her and giving Amelia a nod.

"My dear young one," said Minna, using her accent carefully. "How are you? What a pretty gown, is it from Paris?"

Amelia brightened a little. "Oh, no, it is from Papa's warehouse, and made up by me and our maid!" She blushed, fingering the blue fabric deprecatingly.

45

"But you are so clevair-r-r," murmured Minna. "It does look French! And the silk fabric—from Lyon, yes?"

"Oh, I do believe it is, you are very smart, madam!"

"It is nothing. Well, well, why are you in a corner, Miss Lavery?"

"I'm not Miss Lavery," she said seriously. "That is my eldest sister, Mary. I'm just Amelia."

"Well, just Amelia, why are you in a corner, instead of dancing with one of these so-nice young men?" Minna smiled sweetly at the blushing girl, and tapped her hand with the Spanish fan. "Don't tell me—you are secretly in love with some impossible handsome guardsman, and cannot endure to dance with any nice ordinary young man, eh?"

Amelia giggled. "Oh, no, Madame Dubois. It's just that I cannot dance very well—and I am embarrassed—"

"And how do you expect to dance better—if you do not dance, eh?" asked Minna with French practicality. An echo of Gabrielle's brisk voice came to her, she could just hear the girl scolding her cousin! And yes, she had, in the old days. She had scolded Minna for not trying to dance, for not talking up, for not finding topics of conversation with which to amuse young beaux.

"Well—you may be right—but I stumbled over Mr. Seymour's feet," she said in a rush. "And I knocked an ice from Lady Olive's hand, and it fell on the floor—and I just rushed away. I wish I could go home." And her pretty face crumpled up at the memory.

"Oh, tush, tush. The footman got it up at once, I am sure. What a tragedy," scolded Minna softly. It was a tragedy to a sensitive young girl, she knew by experience. But one must make light of it. "Do you suppose you are the only one who has done that? I remember when I was fifteen, Mother asked me to serve tea for her, and I was so shaky I spilled a cup all over the trousers of a professor! I could have died!"

"Oh, what did you do?"

"I wanted to rush away. But Mother rang for a maid, we mopped it up, the professor forgave me nicely when I quoted some German scholar to him on my father's urging. He said one could forgive a girl who used her mind, and I would learn grace with age! He was really very sweet to me."

"Your parents do sound nice, did you live in Paris always?" asked Amelia curiously, and Minna realized she was in danger. She had told an experience of Minna and not of Gabrielle!

"Not always, no, we lived in the country some miles south. And during the war, I lived with my cousins in Kent for some three years. They were most kind to me, veree gracious—"

Ten minutes had passed. Teddy Bailey, red-faced and looking anxious, was shyly approaching them.

Minna leaned to the girl and whispered, "Here comes that nice Mr. Bailey. If he asks you to dance, smile and do dance with him. He is more shy than you are, I do believe! Such a sweet man!"

Teddy came to them, fixed his eyes on Amelia desperately, and blurted, "May I ha-have this d-d-dance, Miss Amelia?"

She swallowed, and held out her hand. He helped her up, and they moved away. "W-what a nice p-party," said Amelia as they moved into the ballroom.

"Very nicely done, Madame Dubois," said a low voice from beside Minna.

She started, turning about with a jerk of her shoulders. Oliver Seymour stood near to her, so close he must have heard what had transpired.

"Oh—you heard?"

"Yes, it was very kind-hearted of you to encourage the child—and Teddy," he said gravely. "You know, I was about to write you off as a French jade, a flirt, but now I think you must be as good as you are beautiful," and his gray eyes looked at her very intently.

She tried to laugh, her cheeks felt warm. "What a wicked thing to say to me, *monsieur!*" She tried to scold him. "A French jade, indeed! That is wicked!"

"Tell me I am forgiven, and you will come for a drive with me tomorrow in my carriage. May I call for you— about eleven?"

Oh, he was falling at her feet! She felt jubilant, and could scarcely conceal her pleasure. She let her eyelashes droop.

"Why, I am not sure—let me see, it is Saturday— I wonder if *ma chère tante* has any engagements—"

"She does not, I have asked her. She gives her permission for you to come with me in the park. I have a new team of matched blacks, I think you will enjoy them—"

His matched blacks! She had longed to see them, and now he was inviting her to come and not only see them, but ride behind them. Her heart surged with pleasure. She loved fine horses, and he had the money to buy the best.

"If *Tante* says that I may—perhaps it will be all

right—although I did think someone was coming to tea—" She said it demurely.

Oliver said fiercely, "I will not let any engagements stand in my way! You will come!"

"Dear me, *monsieur,* you are so—persuasive!" A look up at him, a half smile, and he was bending to her.

"I have done four duty dances, now I have returned for my reward," he said, and held out his hand to her. She let him draw her up from the chair, and put his right arm about her, to lead her into the next dance.

She was very conscious of Astrid's cold eyes following them as they danced. The young girl stood at the side of the room, tearing up her fan as Minna danced again and again with Oliver. Good! That was sweet revenge, and Minna laughed and flirted with her eyes at Oliver.

She went in to supper with him, he seated her and brought offerings to her of the many delicacies of the buffet—cold chicken and ham rolled in herb dressing, chilled jellies, spicy hot fish pie, cold dressed crab, potted lobster. She could not eat all he brought, and laughingly protested when he went back yet again to bring her another dish of tempting delights.

He insisted, she must eat some of the orange trifle, the iced sweet cherry pudding, the whim-wham made with thick cream and candied orange peel, the almond sugar puffs. And he had a footman bring several times trays of chilled glasses of sparkling champagne just for them.

After the collation, there was dancing yet again. The older folks began to weary and began to drift to the door, the young ones kept on vigorously dancing.

Minna was beginning to tire herself, she found the

49

French accent and masquerade a bit difficult to carry on for many hours. But Oliver would not let her depart.

He swept her into the flower conservatory toward the end of the evening, and she leaned gratefully in the coolness to get whiffs of the forced roses and violets, the carnations and little pinks, the rare orchids hanging from thin vines.

"How lovely," she said naturally. "You are most fortunate to have such a paradise in your beautiful home."

"A paradise is empty without its angel," he said in a strained voice, and took her in his arms.

She was so surprised that she did not fight. Besides, Gabrielle would not have fought! He held her with his hard muscular arms, and pressed a kiss on her parted lips. She gasped, and he kissed her again, her soft mouth was crushed beneath his urgent champagne-laden lips. She tasted the wine on his lips, and wondered vaguely if he tasted hers in the same way.

His one hand went to her hips, and pressed her roughly to his thighs. He was very excited and hot, she felt the hard thighs against her soft hips, felt something very hard and urgent pressing on her.

"You—darling," he said hoarsely, and his lips went roving over her soft throat to her pulse beating madly. Then his mouth lingered at the pulse beat, seeming to drink of it. "You feel for me also—you knew—when our eyes first met—oh, God, I am mad for you—"

Minerva could not think at all. He had her lying over his powerful arm, he had her bent back against the work table in the flower conservatory. She thought faintly that she might knock over a few pots, and then would the gardeners be furious!

The scent of roses in her nostrils, and his male
50

scent—hot, awakened ardor, and the pressure of his body against her silk gown and her thighs— What was he doing, he kept pressing harder to her—

One of her hands groped for his shoulder, to keep herself from falling backwards onto the work table. She gripped his silk-clad shoulder, and felt the hardness of it. How men felt—she had never known how hard they were, compared to the soft feel of a girl like herself. Was their skin also hard and rough? She put her other hand involuntarily to his cheek, and yes, it was rough a bit, from the beginning of a scratchy beard—he must have shaved in the afternoon—and now his skin was roughened, and he scratched her cheek when he pressed his cheek to hers.

"You are—adorable," he muttered against her throat, and his lips roamed lower, until he pressed them to the valley between her rounded breasts. She felt his lips against the side of her breast, the greedy searching of his mouth for the taut nipple—

Oh, God, she must not let him. But it was so sweet a touch, so fiery and unexpected— She groaned in her throat, and he heard her, and raised his head.

"You want me also!" he said triumphantly. Then his mouth closed over her opened mouth, and his tongue went between her lips. She felt as though he had invaded her flesh, and she stiffened and began to fight him.

It did no good, he was much stronger than she. And for a few moments he went on kissing her hotly, wildly, his mouth opened against hers, his tongue thrusting about in her mouth, searching, finding, teasing, thrusting.

Voices nearby, someone's laughter. He straightened

abruptly, and let her up, his arm still about her. He looked down at her, his eyes blazing in the dimness of the conservatory.

"Not now," he said, and it was a promise. "Not now—Gabrielle!"

It was like a slap, like a fling of cold water in her face. Gabrielle! Of course, the French jade! She gasped, and put her hands to her face, and fought to get herself under control.

"I must—g-go," she said wildly. "I have to—g-go and f-find—"

"I'll take you to your aunt," he said swiftly. His hands went to her hair, smoothed it awkwardly, his hands lingering on the silken curls, the little wisps of fly-away reddish gold hair. "Don't worry—you look a bit flushed. Come along."

Gently he put his arm in hers, and led her from the room. A few eagerly curious guests followed their progress with their gazes, but many had left, the rooms were almost empty.

She found her mother, and Betsy Redmond looked at them both with worry in her eyes. "Here is your niece," said Oliver gaily, a red flush high on his cheekbones. "She is going riding with me tomorrow at eleven."

Minna made a sound in her throat; he looked down at her.

"You *are*," he said, softly, ominously, his gray eyes a bright threat. "By the way, how is Minna? You said she is ill?"

"Yes—with a fever," Minna managed, past the obstruction in her throat. She did feel very feverish!

"Too bad—pray give her my regards," he said indifferently.

Oh, he would pay for that! That cool indifference, for poor sick Minna!

In the carriage going home, Minna was very silent. Her mother glanced at her from time to time, trouble in her look.

How bold he had been, how very bold and forward! She should have hit him! She should have given him a tongue-lashing! But her mouth still stung softly from his passion, and her body remembered his pressure against it.

Dreamily she smiled out the window at the cool night air, at the darkness, with few stars visible.

In bed that night, she was a long time getting to sleep. She kept thinking about Oliver. He had been very bold, very wicked!

But oh—she had liked it! No wonder girls like Gabrielle had hidden in bushes with young men, and let themselves be kissed! Minna had not known what she was missing. She touched her lips with her fingers, and shut her eyes tight, to bring back the memory of his mouth on hers, his tongue pressing her tongue. And the way he had kissed her all down her body—as far as he could go!

Wicked! But delicious!

Chapter 4

IN SPITE OF the late hour at which he had retired, Oliver Seymour was up early the next day. He dressed with care in a new riding suit of green and gold, fussed at his valet over his hair arrangement, and finally set out half an hour early with his carriage and matched black stallions.

He could not wait to see Madame Dubois again! How glorious she was! He had never met anyone so exciting and passionate, with such a sense of humor, such sweetness, and her lips! Oh, God, her lips and her silky skin—

She was a close relation of the Redmonds, or he would have thought her fast, and ready to be set up as a mistress. How bold she was, her eyes so flirtatious and inviting! And allowing him to kiss her the first evening! He wondered—would she allow him to set her up in a flat? He had never felt so excited by a female! He had never had a permanent mistress, but Madame Dubois was different! She was a widow—perhaps she was highly sexed, and missed her husband! Or perhaps she had had a French lover!

He drew up in front of the modest London townhouse of the Redmonds. The footman came out to hold the restless horses—fortunately Oliver trusted their servants. He went to the door eagerly, and was let in.

"Madame Dubois is not yet down, sir," said the butler, dubiously, and showed him into the empty drawing room.

He waited, cooling his heels for quite half an hour, but he knew it was his fault. He was very early.

When the door opened, he turned eagerly, then gasped. Madame Dubois came in, a stunning sight. She wore a slim-fitting black riding habit, with shiny black boots. But on her head was no high black hat.

Her hair was dressed in a multitude of curls and tendrils floating about her charming oval face. On the hair was set a black lace Spanish mantilla, so that the red-gold silk of her hair shone through the black lace. Oh, God, she was so lovely, he thought, as he strode forward to take her gloved hand.

She wore short, tight black gloves. He pushed back the glove so he might press a kiss on the white wrist. When he stood erect, she was surveying him with half-closed eyes, seriously, though her green eyes sparkled.

"You are most early, dear sir," she murmured. "I regret my lateness—I was not dressed."

Oliver had a quick mental picture of her, half awake, yawning and stretching out her white arm in a vast bed, clothed in a lace confection which showed her beautiful skin. Perhaps a black lace nightdress—and her white breasts glimmering from the lace—

"I would you had allowed me to come up and share your morning coffee," he said daringly.

Some color crept into her painted cheeks. He did not like the fashion of rouge and powder, but he had to confess it was becoming on her. And that black stuff on her eyelashes—it brought out the green of her eyes. What magnificent eyes she had, they were so expressive—

"You are being wicked this morning," she scolded, and tapped his hand lightly with her gloved fingers. "I do not know if I should allow you to take me out!"

"You promised!"

He took her arm so she could not get away. She laughed lightly, a gurgle of low sound in the long slim throat. She permitted him to take her into the hallway, and out into the morning sunlight of the April day. What a glorious day! What a beautiful London-town! He walked on air, as he handed her up into the carriage.

As he swung up, he remembered his manners. "Your aunt—she is well?"

"Yes, but sleeping late today, after our late night," she said lightly. "How we enjoyed ourselves last night! Your entertainment is superb!"

"I thank you." He was inordinately pleased with her compliment. "And your cousin, Minerva? She is well?"

She gave him a quick reproachful look. "Oh, no, alas, *monsieur,* she is most ill, wiz the fever, you comprehend! The doctor will be called again this afternoon. Poor child, how she suffers! I should have stayed with her, but one is not permitted to enter the room!"

"Oh—too bad," he murmured, feeling a little pang, for he was so happy he wanted everyone in the world to be happy today. She was sitting close beside him on the seat of the carriage; he could see, from the corner of his eye, her graceful movements as she swayed to the movement of the carriage.

How glorious her form! Rounded and slim in the waist, her body was so pleasing—her hips were wide and rounded, he had felt them with his hands when he had embraced her last night. No slim-stick was she!

56

Her breasts were globes of delight, round and white and tempting—

"How beautiful are your stallions—do I say it right, stallions?" And she looked up at him, and curled her red tongue around the word. He could scarce look away to pay attention to his spirited horses, he swallowed. He wanted to grasp her, and plunge his mouth onto her mouth and kiss her senseless!

"Yes, right," he gasped. "Do you like—horses?"

"I do not know much about zem," she said seriously. "My 'usband, Gaspar, he chose our horses for us, and looked about the stables—he did not permit me to do such things as ride. It was not—feminine, he said."

This was confirming what he had thought, her marriage had not been a happy one. Shadows filled her expressive green eyes when she spoke of Gaspar. And he must have been a bossy brute!

"Should you like to ride? I would enjoy teaching you—" he offered eagerly.

"Oh, I shall not be in London long enough—I do zank you for your kindness, though," and she gazed up into his eyes so deeply that the horses strayed into the next path.

On someone's warning shout, he jerked the reins, and got himself under control, and then the horses. His face flushed with embarrassment. He counted himself a tolerable whip, but today he was off his pace!

Gabrielle did not seem to notice, she was gazing off into the distance across the park as they entered the grounds. He did not like it that she ignored him, that her gaze was elsewhere and her mind seemingly preoccupied with her thoughts.

"Gabrielle!" he urged.

"*Monsieur?*" she murmured, and turned her head slowly back to him. The wind picked up the ends of the Spanish mantilla and floated a bit of lace and some locks of red-gold hair, it was a delicious sight.

"I wish you would remain longer—what calls you back to France?" he demanded.

"Oh—I have affairs to put in order." She smiled, and showed entrancing white teeth like small pearls.

"Affairs?" For a jealous moment, he thought of some young dandy of a Frenchman.

"Yes, financial," she said demurely. "What did you think? There is the estate—though most belongs to my stepson—he is about my age, you know."

Oliver frowned. He did not like the thought of a stepson her own age!

"He is married?" demanded Oliver.

"Yes, how did you know?"

"I guessed." Those young Frenchies, they liked to have their wives, and a mistress or two on the side. Surely that young dandy would not dare approach his own stepmother—

"Then, in May, Paris is so very pretteee," she was saying. "I long to return to my Paris when the chestnuts are in blossom along the lovely *boulevards*—and everyone is out in the parks—oh, do we know that gentleman?"

Oliver looked. "Yes, I introduced you last night—" Curtly he nodded as Gabrielle waved and smiled.

The gentleman galloped up, and stopped them to talk for a moment. Oliver was furious, and glared at him. Gabrielle was too free with her smiles and her pretty talk.

But soon he was able to drive on. Then someone else

waved his riding crop, and they had to stop and talk again.

"No more," said Oliver, as he drove away this time. "I shall not stop again! I wanted you to myself this morning! There are too many people in the world!"

Her lovely eyes opened wide in mock amazement. "Oh, *monsieur*, you theenk so? You wish to speak seriously about ze problems of ze world to me?"

"No, I do not, and you know it! I wish I could be alone with you. You are the most beautiful woman in the world—I cannot wait to kiss you again!"

She shook her head, and the red-gold hair waved against his arm. "You were very—forward last night, *monsieur*. I was wrong to permit you to take me to the conservatory. No, it was wrong."

She rebuked him, yet her green eyes sparkled up at him, and a little smile curled her red-paste mouth. She wore too much makeup, yet she was so pretty in spite of it—

"I think you are not angry with me—" he said softly, "because you enjoyed it almost as much as I did! I think you miss kisses and embraces. I think you hunger for the love of a strong man! And I would be that man in your life!"

She turned her head away, to greet someone else, and he was furious! He would not stop the carriage, and the ladies in the other carriage stared after him as he whipped the horses and turned them into yet another graveled path.

"I am determined to talk alone with you!" he growled.

"*Monsieur!* You go too fast," she said, her head still turned from him.

59

"If you think to leave London, I will not permit it! I long to know you better— Do you not feel, Gabrielle, that there is something special between us? From the first moment that we met, when our eyes first met, I knew there was something unusual between us, that we were destined to know each other well. I have never felt toward another woman what I have felt for you. And when I kissed you—"

"'Ow do you do?" Gabrielle said clearly, and bowed to a gentleman on horseback. He paused, smiled, was eager to continue.

Oliver sent the horses flying on, even faster.

"I said, when I kissed you last night—I felt such emotion—I have never felt so about any female—"

"I zink we must forget last night, it was a mistake!"

"A mistake!" He gasped. "No! It was right, the first right move I have made toward a female—I think I am falling in love with you—deeply in love!"

"*Monsieur,* you must forget me!"

"Why?" he demanded.

She was silent. He wished his hands were not full of the reins, and trying to control two very spirited stallions.

"Is there someone else?" he asked again.

She did not answer.

He could have cursed. He felt so dazzled, so confused, so irritated by the horses and the public nature of their meeting. If only he had been smart enough to take her to his home. But she would not have come—unless—

"May I take you to my house for luncheon, so we may continue this conversation?" he begged.

"No, I must return home—to *ma tante*'s house," she
60

said firmly. "I promised I will come home at one or before. What time is it?"

He glanced at his gold turnip watch on his waistcoat. "Five until one." He groaned, then wished he had lied.

"Then we must return home," she said calmly. Reluctantly he turned the horses, and all too soon, he was pulling up in front of the Redmond townhouse.

And to his amazed disgust, the footman came out— with Percival Redmond.

"Percival!" cried his passenger, with every evidence of joy. "You have come to London—you have deserted Kent, and come to London! Oh, I am so happee!"

Percival Redmond, looking rather grim, assisted her in alighting, and was glaring up at Oliver. "How are you, Mr. Seymour," he said formally.

Oliver was trapped with his horses and reins. "Splendid to see you, Percival," he muttered. "I say, Madame Dubois—will you come for dinner this evening?"

"Oh, no," she said clearly. "Percy has just come! We cannot!"

"Then tomorrow?" he cried in despair, as she began to move to the house, her hand tucked cozily in Percy's arm.

"Not tomorrow!" said Percy firmly. He was frowning.

"On Monday, then?" Oliver felt like a sapskull as he sat in the carriage and yelled pleadingly after them.

"Come to tea on Monday afternoon," called Gabrielle, and sent him a dazzling smile.

"Oh, thank you!" he answered, like a very hopeless lover. The footman could scarce conceal his grin, and Oliver picked up his reins to chirrup at the horses, feeling very cross.

Percival yanked Minerva into the house, then in to the front drawing room, and shut the doors after them.

"Now, what the devil are you up to, Minerva?" he asked grimly, standing with his hands on his hips, and looking more formidable than usual.

"However did you happen to come to London?" she asked, sinking into the nearest chair. Her mother was lounging in the armchair near the tea tray, looking thoughtful and pensive.

"Mother sent for me," he answered.

Minna looked at her mother reproachfully. Betsy Redmond shrugged. "I thought you should have an escort," she evaded.

"But Percy is busy with the farm," protested Minna, and set back the black veil. She thought the morning had been quite a success, and she had wanted to gloat over it, and how fast Oliver was falling. He had practically declared himself today! Her heart was beating rapidly, she did not want to fight with Percy just now. She wanted to go up to her room and savor the morning's experiences.

"Well—I wanted to see Denise Lavery," said Percy, with unusual bluntness. "Mother said also that Ross Harmsworth is hanging about her too much. I want to marry her, and I won't be cut out by that—that—"

"That handsome soldier," said Minerva sweetly. "Yes, he is hanging about her. But if you neglect her from one season to the next, I cannot blame her for looking to someone else!"

"Minerva," said her mother warningly. "Percy is genuinely fond of Denise—and he works hard—"

"Yes, Mother. But women want to know they come first," said Minna.

62

Both her brother and mother stared at Minna. She realized it was not one of her usual statements, and blushed.

"Well, matters are going well on the farm," said Percy, pacing to the window and back again. He did look tired and harassed, thought his sister fondly. He did need a holiday. "I thought I would come up to London for a few weeks, and press my courtship. This is her second season, after all. She should be satisfied to cut a swathe and be done with it!"

Minerva raised her eyebrows. "What a way to put it," she said. "Denise is a good, kind girl. Why should she not have a good time this season? She deserves to be happy."

"Of course, of course," said Percy. "But she liked me well enough last season. Why hasn't she written to me?" he blurted out.

Minna and her mother exchanged another look. So Percy had written to Denise, but not received many answers. Maybe Denise was serious about Harmsworth—or maybe she just wanted more attention than Percy had had time to give her.

"Well, well, you must give up this masquerade," Percy continued. "I will want you to come about with Denise and me, it will only be proper. Perhaps we can be engaged by next month," he added hopefully.

Minna did not like this at all. She was having a splendid time, being reckless Gabrielle instead of staid Minerva. "But, Percy, I am in the midst of this scheme of mine, didn't Mother tell you?"

"She said something about you were mad as fire at Oliver Seymour. I cannot understand why."

"He insulted me," she said.

Percy went stiff as a poker. "He—insulted you?" he asked, in a deadly tone.

"I mean—he said things to me—about me—"

"How did you come to hear this?"

"I was listening—I mean—"

"What did he say? Did he speak of you as a loose woman? I cannot imagine this of Oliver! He always seemed a courteous chap."

Percy seemed to be taking this wrong. Minna eyed him uneasily. "Well, he insulted me, and I did hear him. I shall not be satisfied until I have my revenge on him! I mean to see him at my feet!"

Percy stood still, his hands behind his back, frowning heavily. The frown looked ill on his fresh, young, open face. He was but twenty-four years of age, about Oliver's height, but not with his years or experience. He had green eyes like Minerva and his mother, red hair a little darker than hers. But his responsibilities had made him grave before his time.

A surge of love for her brother went over Minerva. He was a splendid fellow, and he deserved a good, kind wife, like Denise. What was wrong with Denise, that she could not see his worth?

Perhaps a bit of flirting with Percy was in order! After all, he and "Gabrielle" were only first cousins, and Denise might perk up if she saw Percy hanging about his beautiful widowed cousin!

Percy had other matters on his mind. "If Seymour has insulted you seriously," he said heavily, "then it is up to me to avenge you. I am your only male relative. I shall have to call him out."

"Call him out!" exclaimed Betsy Redmond, sitting

up from her lounging position. "Nonsense— It is not so serious—"

"Now, Percy, that is nonsense," echoed Minna, in alarm. She knew that determined look on her brother's face. "He insulted me, but not like that—I mean—"

"Well, how did he insult you, then?" Percy demanded crossly. "What did he say?"

"He—he called me dull, and dowdy, and dour," muttered Minerva sulkily. The memory still stung badly.

Percy stared at her. "Is that all? Is that what has you in such a pother?" he asked, furious. "You mean, I came all the way from Kent to hear this? Mother, really, what did you mean by sending for me as though there was vast trouble?"

"Well, I think it was bad enough!" cried Minerva. "How would you like Denise to think you were dull and dowdy and dour?"

"Is Oliver serious about you? Has he offered for your hand?" demanded Percy. "Are you in love with him? No? Then why do you care what he thinks?"

At the sudden attack, Minna could not think what to say. Her mother intervened hastily.

"Minna is right to feel insulted. She has known Mr. Seymour for some time, as a casual friend. For him to consider her so unworthy of the attentions of a man must surely be insulting to her. As you can see—" Betsy waved her hand at her daughter, "as Gabrielle she can feel free to look different, to act different."

"I knew her at once," said Percy callously. "What is so different? I have seen her in that riding habit a hundred times."

"Her hair is different. She wears rouge and paint like a Frenchwoman," said her mother loyally. "She looks and feels different. And Mr. Seymour seems to treat her differently—"

"Quite differently," snapped Minerva, remembering the morning ride. "I shall give him a run for the money! And when I have him at my feet—"

Percy groaned. "Females are impossible!" he said sweepingly. "I can only hope Denise is not such a little baggage!"

"She probably is," muttered Minerva, a plan forming in her mind. "Percy, if you will help me, I shall help you!"

He eyed her warily. "Why should I agree? I need no help!"

"Yes, you do, with Denise. You shall escort me about, and arouse Oliver Seymour's jealousy. I could see he was already suspicious of you this noon. And I shall do the same for you with Denise! When you escort me in her sight, I shall languish and cast up my eyes, like this—" And she demonstrated, rolling her eyes at him. "And she will be madly jealous, and more interested in you!"

"I don't see why, seeing you are my sister," said Percy, frowning crossly. "It is all a hum!"

"Yes, but she won't know it! I am your cousin Gabrielle, from France, a fascinating widow, and you can escort me devotedly, and make her jealous!" urged Minerva. "Then, when all is right again, Gabrielle can return to France!"

"I cannot see that it will help—"

"I think you might do as your sister wishes for once, Percy," said Betsy Redmond with unusual firmness. "I have another idea also—" Then she lapsed into silence, realizing the two were not listening to her. But she was thoughtful, mulling over some idea.

"Well, whether I help you with Denise Lavery or not, I think you ought to help me for a few days!" announced Minerva crossly. "Oliver Seymour is interested in me. He almost proposed this morning!"

"Proposed! Is he so serious?" asked Percy dubiously.

"Well—he is fascinated. And I want to cast my net wider, and pull him in tighter," said Minna, with reckless disregard for correct fishing terms. She was thinking to herself that Denise needed shaking up also, and a bit of clever fishing on Percy's part. Percy was a great fellow, and Denise could use some heavy competition to make her realize she could lose Percy if she played fast and loose with him.

"Well, if you want Seymour—he is a decent fellow, and you could do worse than marry him," said Percy.

"I don't mean to marry him! I just want—" But Minna, pausing, realized her brother was not listening, and she herself felt uncertain. Did she not want to marry him? Did she want only revenge on Oliver? Or—or had his kisses stirred something in herself, something previously unawakened, and unthought of?

"I think I shall call on Denise tomorrow afternoon," Percy said, striding up and down the carpet. "I have not seen her for a time. Shall I be received, do you think?"

"I shall send her a note, and her mother, and invite them here tomorrow afternoon. That will do better," said Betsy Redmond firmly. "If you go there, they might not be at home. Yes, I shall invite them here."

"Why not invite the whole family, and also Teddy

67

Bailey and Ross Harmsworth?" suggested Minerva cunningly. "I have a plan—I think it might work—"

"I don't want that Harmsworth here," said Percy crossly.

"Just the Laverys tomorrow, dear," pleaded Betsy Redmond. "I shall send a note at once."

And she went to her writing desk, with determination. Minna went upstairs to change for luncheon, and dream a little of her very satisfactory morning. Other plans could wait.

Chapter 5

MINERVA WAS delighted with her new popularity. The Laverys treated her with new respect, she was a favorite of the girls. Denise glared at her suspiciously when Minerva commanded Percy to bring tea, or serve cakes, or pick up something she had dropped.

Yes, it was going so well!

When, on Monday morning, Betsy Redmond suggested that they pay a visit to the dressmaker, Miss Clothilde, Minerva assented like a lamb. At the shop, she pored over lengths of shimmering silks, as Percy sulked in a corner.

"Oh, this is gorgeous," she gasped over a green silk with thin lines of gold. "This will make a stunning ball gown, with cream lace—"

It was ordered, and the dressmaker set several of her little girls to working furiously so the gown could be ready by Wednesday evening, for the select ball at the home of Lady Blanche Villiers.

Then Minerva went on recklessly, encouraged by her mother, to choose a length of silver gray and green stripe for a morning gown, a pink rose confection for evening, an electric blue gown that set off her red hair like fire, a daffodil yellow that made her look like a tea rose, and a sleek gold silk that was so sophisticated Minerva was in ecstasy.

They arrived home to find Oliver Seymour cooling his heels in the drawing room.

"Oh, I am so sorree to keep you waiting," she cried, letting him kiss her hand. He seemed to eat it up, nibbling at the fingers, and she felt a thrill go through her.

"Where have you been?" he asked sharply, as though he had a right to know.

"Buying gowns." She sighed, as though the whole thing fatigued her. "I had not meant to remain so long in London, so I must have more gowns for all the parties. Everyone is too kind to me, I am invited everywhere!"

He looked irritated, yet fascinated, as she left the room to go and remove her hat, renew her makeup, brush out her shining hair, and return to entertain him. She kept him at a little distance, chattered gaily about all her sweet friends in London, how she missed Paris and her friends there, and so on. By the time he left, lingering for quite two hours, she knew he was falling at her feet.

By Wednesday the green silk and lace confection was ready, and she donned it happily. It was so low cut, she felt embarrassed, and averted her eyes from the mirror. But it was all the fashion for married women and widows. Her rounded breasts showed through the cream lace, boldly.

"Has your mother seen this gown?" asked Jessie bluntly, as she arranged the shoulders carefully, trying to bring up the fabric to cover a little more of Minerva.

"Yes, at the dressmaker's when I had a fitting yesterday."

"Well, all I can say is, I'm glad your brother will be there to defend your honor!"

"Now, Jessie," said Minerva. "After all, I am a French widow, and everybody expects me to be fast!"

"Fast is as fast does," muttered Jessie. "Just don't you go out in the garden with no gentlemen!" Jessie arranged the hair curls down on one white shoulder, and fastened a jade butterfly into the fall of curls near her right ear.

"Now, where did this come from, miss?" she asked, curious.

"Mr. Seymour sent it to me with some flowers." Minerva blushed. It had been a surprise, this dainty gift in the box of forced roses, all of beautiful golden yellow. "He is very fond of jade."

"Um. And what did your mother say?"

"She approved. It is not like a precious jewel, she said."

"Hum. Accepting presents from gents, and all. No good can come of it." And Jessie grumped and harrumped the rest of the hour as she finished dressing Minna.

The butterfly was the first thing Oliver Seymour noticed when he rushed to the door to greet her as she entered with her mother and Percy. "You are here— and you wear my gift," he panted, taking her hand reverently, and pressing a kiss on it. His gray eyes glowed as he looked her over from head to foot, and she felt sure he did not miss her bosom.

"'Ow do you do, Mr. Seymour?" she said demurely. "I must greet my hostess," and she drew her hand slowly from his to turn to the lady who stood nearby, watching the scene thoughtfully. "Lady Villiers, 'ow nice of you to invite me. My cousin Minerva Redmond sends her apologies, she is still so veree sick—"

"I am so sorry to hear, pray give her my best regards," said Lady Blanche Villiers. "And so you are their French cousin? You have some resemblance to Minerva, I believe."

"Oh, yes, we are first cousins," smiled "Gabrielle." "But Minerva is much more clever than I, she likes to read ze books ze best. Me, I like ze—people!" she proclaimed, and smiled alluringly up at Oliver Seymour, close at her side.

Betsy Redmond choked a little, covered it with her hand, and greeted her hostess with exquisite manners. Percy was exclaimed over, and told he was handsomer than ever, then they were allowed to pass on to the drawing room. Percy was clinging to Minerva on one side, and his mother on the other. Oliver glared at him.

Percy did not approve of Minerva's new gown, nor her heavy makeup, nor her accent, nor her masquerade. Gloomily he surveyed the room, located Denise Lavery in a pale blue gown that made her look like a demure shepherdess, and sighed.

"I will take care of Madame Dubois," said Oliver, definitely. "You need not linger, Percy!"

"What? Oh. No, I am my—cousin's escort. I shall look after her," said Percy, just as firmly. He had told Minerva he was sure she would be insulted tonight, and deserved it, for such a low-cut gown.

Oliver frowned. "I do not see that you need worry about your cousin. Why don't you go off and attend Miss Lavery?"

"She is well attended," said Percy, glaring at Ross

72

Harmsworth, who now swept Denise Lavery into a dance.

Hastily Minerva turned to Oliver. "Do ask me to dance," she whispered.

He was not slow in doing so, and put his arm possessively about her, to lead her into the next set. Percy glared after them.

"I am sure he is fond of the pretty little Miss Lavery," murmured Minerva. "But he is so—fond of me—that he worries between his duty to me and his wish to be—wiz her." Her eyelashes dropped.

"I cannot approve of marriages between first cousins," proclaimed Oliver boldly.

Minerva opened her eyes widely, gazing up at him. "Marriage? Who spoke of marriage, *monsieur?*"

"Or affairs!" he continued.

"Non, non, not affairs," she agreed sweetly. "That would be naughty, no?"

"Have you had affairs, *madame?*"

"Monsieur!" she scolded. And then she giggled. "What a question. I thought Englishmen were so staid!"

"We are not all staid, Gabrielle!" he murmured into her hair, and she felt a quick kiss on her white forehead. Then he stood erect once more, leading her into the next move. He had to let her go to another man in the set, but when he returned to her, he said, "You did not answer my question."

"Which question, *monsieur?* You ask so many!"

"You tease me all the time," he growled in a low voice.

She giggled again, and he gazed down into her animated face with a sort of hungry look that reminded her of a black panther she had once seen in a cage in the zoological gardens. Tail swishing, pace slow, muscles rippling along the black hide, as though he longed to spring—

The dance ended. Ross Harmsworth was there, in an instant, and claimed her hand. Oliver frowned. "She is with me," he proclaimed.

"Oh, I say, Seymour, not twice in a row," protested Harmsworth with a smile, and carried off Minerva triumphantly.

Oliver glared after them, not seeing Astrid Faversham, who stood hopefully nearby. He waited until the set ended, then grabbed Minerva's hand once more.

"Oh, I promised this to Percy," she said innocently, and pretended to look about for him.

"He is busy with Denise Lavery, do not interrupt them!" advised Oliver, and swept her into the waltz. "I have asked for this waltz from the orchestra—you dance it so divinely!"

"Zank you—you are so kind—" She did not say she had never danced it as she did with Oliver. She felt swept in his arms with a divine frenzy, she wanted to dance and kick up her heels, and let him swing her right off the floor with his strong arm. How sweetly delicious to waltz with him! He was so powerful, so demanding, so passionate!

"Have you been in the home of Lady Villiers before?" he asked as the dance ended.

"Oh, yes, several times," she replied, before recalling that "Gabrielle" had not. But he did not know the difference.

Oliver frowned. "And I suppose gentlemen have always taken you to her conservatory?"

"No, I have not seen her conservatory," said Mi-

74

nerva, daringly. She knew where he was leading. Yet she went along gladly, heart thumping.

He took her to the large, green-walled room in glass at the end of a long corridor. They passed some fine furniture; she did not note it. They passed cabinets of fine china and glass; she did not see it. But in the end room he opened the painted blue door, and ushered her into a warm, steamy, glass room, in which were set shelves of pots—roses, orchids, exotic oriental flowers in gay colors.

"How lovely," she exclaimed, and started to examine the blooms. "This rose is very beautiful—such a deep rose color—"

Oliver paid no attention. He had his arm about her, he turned her to him. "I have waited for days for this," he said thickly, and bent his head.

He was so abrupt, he took her by complete surprise. On her half-opened mouth, he pressed his lips, and the hot passion of his mouth surprised her into silence. He bent her back, urgently, and his body pressed against her slim, rounded form, as though he would imprint himself on her.

She had thought to keep control of the moment, but could not. Warmth swept through her in the warm, steamy room. Her hand crept up to his neck, and her fingers curled about his strong throat. She caressed the scratchy skin where he had shaved, she felt the thick, dark curly hair as it peaked near his neck. How unexpectedly silky was his hair, such thick curls, his son would have hair like that, baby fine.

His mouth pressed more deeply on hers, and his tongue pressed urgently into her mouth, in one of those intimate kisses which made her feel she herself was being invaded. She tried to turn her head aside, but it was so delicious—she yielded, and her mouth opened to his, and her tongue timidly touched his.

He groaned, deep in his throat, and his hands began to sweep over her silk-clad body. He put his hands on her hips, and boldly moved his hands up and over them, and to her waist, up to her back and shoulders, and down again, sweeping up and down, ever pressing her closer to him, so she felt every line and bulge of his hard body. He pressed his thighs to hers, and she could feel the masculinity of him against her softness.

His mouth left hers briefly, to move over her cheek and chin, over to her ear. He nibbled on the lobe, nipped it rather savagely, and she felt erotic sensations sweeping through her.

"God, I wish I could take you right here," he muttered, but she heard him very clearly, and a hot blush swept through her.

She drew back, pushing against his shoulders, but she could not keep his thighs from pressing more firmly on hers. "Sir, you must let me—g-go," she gasped. "I d-did not mean—you must—let me—g-go—p-please!"

"You are adorable," he said huskily, not letting her go. His gray eyes were glazed with passion. "Will you come to my house soon—I must see you alone—"

She wanted him at her feet, not alone in his house. "No, I cannot," she said firmly. "I—I zink you insult me," she invented quickly. "I am not zat kind! You zink because I—I like people—that I would let myself—no, no, I am not zat kind! Is that why you ask about affairs, *monsieur?*"

His arms loosened, she pulled herself away firmly,

76

though he kept his hands on her hips in a familiar manner.

"Then you are just a tease?" he accused. "You do not mean to allow me to—to have you? I tell you—" Then he looked down into her wide eyes, a bit frightened now because he did not let her go.

"I do not have affairs," she affirmed quietly.

He drew a deep shaky breath, and let her go. She stepped back, her skirts sweeping against some dirty pots. "Do not—you will get your gown dirty," he said, and put his hand on her bare arm to draw her away from the pots.

"If one gets near dirt, one gets dirty," she said quaintly. "One should be careful—not to get too near to dirt," and she looked up at him with a straight gaze.

He was flushed, he put his hand ruefully to the back of his neck, and rubbed it in a boyish gesture that went straight to her heart.

"I have—misjudged you, haven't I, Gabrielle?" he asked. "I thought you might—frankly—that you might be willing to let me set you up as my—mistress. I would pay you well, find you a splendid apartment—"

She felt shocked, and gasped, her eyes shocked. Was this what she had brought on herself? This insult? Was her behavior so loose—

"It is my fault," he went on quickly. "I suppose in France the ladies flirt more, they have a different court there—or did, before the Revolution. Society is different there. I have misunderstood you, I think. Forgive me!"

"You are—forgiven—*monsieur*," she said slowly. "But you do misunderstand me. I enjoy people—I enjoy talking wiz men—" And she smiled wistfully, and

77

turned her head away. "The years wiz my Gaspar—I was restless, and foolish, perhaps—" She let him finish the sentence. "I must go back to the ballroom."

She meant to intrigue him, make him guess about her. But she was furious also that he had said that about setting her up as his mistress!

"Don't go!" He caught her arm, tried to hold her back. "We must speak more. What did you mean? Have you had affairs? Gabrielle, I must know—speak frankly, I implore you—"

Minerva had no intention of speaking frankly, and giving her game away. She was angry, yet drawn to him. She had enjoyed his kisses. But he was not going to know just what he could do with "Gabrielle"! Let him guess and stew and wonder! She wanted him abject, and at her feet! She would not be satisfied until he was.

"I must go—it is indiscreet to remain here," she said, and pushed him firmly with her to the door, teasing him, her hand on his broad hard back. She enjoyed the touch of his silky coat, the warmth beneath it. "Come now, do not be obstinate!"

He half laughed, half frowned, but went with her. Inside the first drawing room, they encountered Astrid Faversham with Ross Harmsworth, and Astrid's cold gray eyes were furious!

"Well, well, Madame Dubois and Mr. Seymour! Wherever have you been?" she drawled, and her gaze went significantly to the blue door to the conservatory. "Among the flowers—and the birds and bees and all the nature inside?"

Minerva felt furious, but smiled sweetly, her hand on the stiffened arm of her escort. *"Mais, oui, enfant,"* she said, deliberately. "Just seeing the flowers, of course!" and she swept on, with a laugh.

Astrid raged, her voice too clear, "Oh, she is brazen— that Frenchwoman! She is not fit for English company!"

Oliver made to turn back. Minerva stopped him. "Do not mind her," she said, in a low, placating tone. "She is so foolish, that one. So young and jealous of everyone. Such a bitter little mind, hers!" And she felt that she had triumphed over Astrid, for Oliver nodded and gave the girl a contemptuous look.

"Yes, she does not deserve attention," he said, and went on to the next rooms with Minerva. "May I take you in to supper tonight?"

"Well—yes," she said, with a little laugh. "You do find such delicious foods, and the best desserts!"

"Greedy little lady!" he muttered in her ear, and managed to give the ear a little bite with his teeth. "I wish I could turn that appetite of yours to other— more fascinating desires!"

That was bold indeed, and she should have rebuked him. But they were in the company now, and people were too close.

"Wicked," she muttered, and shook her head at him. But his gray eyes only laughed down into hers, and he seemed to think they were of one mind about that.

She moved near to her mother, and settled down into a chair for a brief rest. Oliver reluctantly left her for some duty dances. Minerva refused the next two men, with a smile, and a wave of her green and gold fan.

"*Non, non,* find some other girl to dance wiz!" She laughed. "I am weary of dancing, I must sit and rest and chat with *ma tante!*"

Astrid Faversham crept closer, listening to her, her

79

sharp eyes searching, searching for a flaw. Minerva smiled serenely, and turned to her mother.

"How do I do?" she muttered.

"My dear, everyone is talking about you and Oliver disappearing for fifteen minutes!" her mother whispered. "You will wreck your reputation completely. And your dress is mussed—there is dirt on the back of the skirt."

"Pots of roses in the conservatory," Minerva muttered, and rose with a smile. "Come to the dressing room with me, and brush me off," she whispered.

They disappeared into the dressing room, where Astrid followed them. Mary Lavery was there, twenty-one, plain, and good. She helped Betsy Redmond brush down Minerva's skirt.

"What a shame to get this gown dirty," said Mary innocently. "However did you do it?"

"Someone was showing her the conservatory," said Astrid sharply, as she pretended to brush her silvery blond hair. "A place I'll warrant you have never seen, except to look at the flowers!"

It was a slap at both Mary, who was plain and not popular with men, and at Minerva, who had disappeared into the conservatory with a man and come out with her gown dirty. And it was overheard by their hostess, Lady Blanche Villiers who had entered the room.

Minerva's quick tongue could not resist the challenge. "Miss Faversham, I fear you are becoming so catty at such an early age, that when you reach the age of a matron you will be much disliked," she said, with quiet dignity. "You must watch what you say, and be more kind, or no one will wish you about."

"Well—really!" gasped Astrid. Lady Blanche nodded her white head.

"She is right, Miss Faversham," she said, in her ringing voice. "Much gossip is spoken in society, to my regret. But when a woman puts herself about to be so catty and deliberately sets out to hurt, that I cannot approve. I pray you will watch your tongue in my house."

And she turned to Mary, and said, "Is the dirt out of the gown? I should send in my maid to do this."

"Oh, thank you, Lady Blanche," said Mary quickly, a flush high on her cheekbones. "I think I have it out. The dirt was quite loose, and dry."

"You are a good, fine girl, and I am sure I thank you," said Lady Blanche. "We are putting on a charity raffle in two weeks, I have been meaning to ask you to be one of my hostesses. It is on May the sixth—do you have time to do this?"

It was a gracious gesture to Mary, for the hostesses were much envied. And it was a cut direct to Astrid, who had coveted the position. Astrid went an unbecoming red, and flounced from the room.

Mary accepted, with a stammer, and Lady Blanche turned to Minerva with a smile.

"I would ask you, Madame Dubois, but as you are a widow, you are not eligible. I only hope your young cousin will recover in time to be one of our hostesses. How is she?"

"She is slow in recovering," said "Gabrielle," feeling rather abashed at the lady's graciousness. "You are kind to ask after her. She will be comforted by your thoughtfulness."

"Pray, take her some of the little cakes, if you think

81

she would enjoy them. I will have a basket prepared for her." And the lady swept from the room.

"Dear me, she is so very kind," said Mary. "I wonder if she really wants me—"

"She asked you, she means it," said Betsy Redmond firmly. "Now, pray, let us return to the ballroom. Gabrielle, my dear, who takes you in to supper? Shall we ask Percy?"

"No, Oliver Seymour has asked me," she said, with a blush she could not control.

"He cannot keep his gaze from you," murmured Mary, with a smile and a significant look.

"You are too kind and you exaggerate," protested Minerva, but she put her arm in Mary's and walked with her back to the ballroom.

She had always liked Mary, and it did not displease her that Astrid Faversham had had a sharp setdown. Altogether a splendid evening, she thought, as Oliver hastened to her, and offered her his arm.

"You will take us both in to supper," she told him gaily, indicating Mary with a smile.

He showed his good manners by being gallant, and bringing plates and wine to them both. Mary talked up in a spirited manner, and showed her intelligence and sense of humor. They all had a lovely time until the dancing began again. Then Oliver managed to get a gentleman to take Mary into the next set, while he repossessed himself of Minerva's hand.

"I could wish you were less kind," he whispered to her. "But I confess I like this side of you! So many lovely ladies have too much cat in them!"

"I think so also!" she said in such a decided way that he gazed down at her in surprise.

Then he put his arm about her, to dance, and they both forgot everyone else in the world.

Chapter 6

ON THURSDAY MORNING, Minerva forced herself to rise early, she must go to the dressmaker's for another fitting. She wanted to lie abed and dream of her conquest!

Oliver Seymour—how handsome and charming, though he had such a wicked tongue. Oh, how she looked forward to having him at her feet! She yawned and stretched in the wide bed, and smiled to herself, thinking of those minutes in the conservatory. How he kissed! How he held her!

"Now, Miss Minerva, it is more than time to rise," said Jessie, observing her shrewdly. "You smile like a cat this morning!"

"Oh, not like a cat, pray!" objected Minerva, stretching. "I have formed an aversion to cats!"

She finally rose, washed, and dressed in Gabrielle's old rose gown, which was such a contrast to her bright red hair. About ten o'clock, after their chocolate, she and her mother and Percy set out for Miss Clothilde's.

They were not the first ones there. The Lavery carriage sat in front of the dressmaker's, and inside they found Denise, Mary, and their mother.

Denise was cool and formal, her violet eyes veiled. Mary was warmly cordial, greeting "Gabrielle" like a long lost relative. Their mother was calm, enjoying the morning, she said, and had not the ball been a delight?

Betsy Redmond agreed with her, and the two matrons settled down for a coz.

"And what gowns will you have made?" asked Mary, with unabashed curiosity of "Gabrielle." "I thought your green jade gown was so beautiful!"

"Thank you, my dear!" Minerva felt years older in her role as the delightful widow Dubois. "You are so kind! Today, I hope several gowns will be finished—a daffodil yellow—a gold silk—"

Mary went with her to see the gowns, and admire as she tried them on. Denise turned her shoulder to the unhappy Percy, and fingered lengths of silk.

"That would be charming on you," said Percy, hopefully, as she picked up a pale violet.

She dropped it, as Minerva watched in the mirror. "Too pale," she said coldly. "It is insipid!"

Percy looked hunted, and retreated to a corner. He was not at his best in the dressmaker's, anyway. Minerva felt furious for him.

"Percy, darling," said Minerva. "Do come and tell me how you like zis dress!" She had put on the gold tissue silk, and it clung all the way down her rounded form.

He came obediently, then his eyes opened wide at sight of his sister in such a dress. "My God, you aren't going to wear that in public?" he asked, startled. "It looks like something from your boudoir!"

Denise jumped visibly. Pleased, Minerva, tapping his cheek, replied, "Now, Percy! That is very naughty of you! Of course, I wear zis in public! It is a ball gown, of the newest French design! Everybody in Paris wears zis style now!"

She did not know it, but they did not either; she felt

quite safe. Miss Clothilde looked a bit peculiar, but her mouth was full of pins, and she said nothing. Only her black eyebrows were raised until they were almost caught in her thick graying black hair.

"I want one like that, Mother," said Denise defiantly.

"Of course not, dear," said practical Charlotte Lavery briskly. "Not until you have been married at least five years!" She and Betsy Redmond exchanged an indulgent look.

"And then I would think your husband would have something to say about that," blurted out Percy. "I think the dress is—is indecent. It shows everything!"

Denise gasped, her eyes huge. She looked up and down Minerva speculatively. "But it does not, Percy!" she said, forgetting her quarrel with him. "She is quite covered!"

"I mean the lines of it," he said. "You can see every line of her—I mean—"

"But it is not nearly so revealing as the gowns we used to wear," cooed Minerva. "Do you remember, *Tante?* When the muslin gowns were dampened with water, to show—all? How everybody stared when we went to balls with those gowns! That style was so stunning!"

"And so conducive to pneumonia," said her mother sharply. "I cannot but be happy that the style is no longer in fashion! It was very foolish!"

"Many styles are foolish," said Minerva with new wisdom. "But if they attract ze men, they do ze purpose, *n'est-ce pas?* A woman dressed to attract ze man she likes, and zat is all ze total of her planning, eh?" And she turned back to the mirror. "Do you zink the neck should be lower, Mademoiselle Clothilde?"

86

Miss Clothilde gave Betsy Redmond a quick look, and shook her head decidedly, without removing the pins from her mouth. She worked earnestly on the hem. Minerva had a shrewd suspicion that the dressmaker was not fooled by her masquerade. The woman had measured her carefully, and blinked when she found that "Madame Dubois" had the exact measurements of Minerva Redmond. But she had said nothing, as usual.

Percy was hanging about his sister anxiously. In a low tone, he said, "I wish you would not buy this gown!"

"Now, Percy," she said gaily, "if you had your way, I would wear a demure black or gray! But I am no longer in mourning!"

"Of course you are not," he said, forgetting himself. Then he scowled. "I mean—you can wear bright colors, but not—not so daring—I beg you!"

Denise was taking this all in, as were Mary and her mother.

Minerva laughed softly, and kissed his cheek. "Dear Percy, how you worry about me! But you must not—I shall manage quite well! And I do love bright colors and new styles!"

He groaned, pushed his hand through his red hair, and went to stand in the window with his back to them all. Denise tightened her mouth, and absently picked up a pallid blue length.

Minerva decided to give the girl another little push. She could see she was jealous and hurt. Well, she should learn to appreciate Percy, and not scorn him.

"That color would be fine for you, Miss Lavery!" she said brightly, carelessly over her shoulder, as she continued to admire herself in the tight golden silk. "The

87

color is pale and demure, just suited to a young girl. This is your first season, yes?"

"My second!" said Denise, in a fierce, smothered tone, and dropped the length. "Mother, I see nothing I like today. Let us depart!"

Denise headed for the door, her mother rising to follow her. Minerva caught Mary's arm as she would have followed.

In a sharp whisper she hissed, "See to it that she does not forget Percy today! I mean to make them a match! But both are stubborn!" And she gave the startled older sister a wink.

"Oh—oh, yes!" gasped Mary, and squeezed Minerva's arm. "I—I shall!"

"And see she comes back and buys some bright, pretty gowns—bright blue—and deep rose—and maybe a red. Percy loves the color of red!"

"I'll do it! You are a dear, Madame Dubois!" And Mary dared to kiss her cheek before she ran after her sister and mother.

Betsy Redmond came closer. "What are you up to?" she asked in a whisper.

"Buying gowns, Mother dearest!" whispered Minerva, then glanced guiltily down at Miss Clothilde at her feet, but the dressmaker pretended not to hear.

They finished the fittings, and Minna went home to lunch, quite satisfied with the day's work in spite of Percy's deep gloom. When men set out to court, they could certainly mess it up, she thought, with new insight.

She coaxed Percy to take her the following morning to the new exhibit of paintings of ocean scenes she wished to see. It was in a gallery near Oliver Seymour's
88

home, and she did not admit even to herself that she hoped to see him.

The silver gray and green stripe had been delivered, and she wore that with a green bonnet set on her flowing red curls.

They wandered from painting to painting. Minerva was so delighted with the beautiful art that she almost forgot her other objective. "Oh, Percy, do admire this one," she said, pausing before a scene of a ship in full sail. "Look at this! How splendid! How I should like to sail away on her!"

"Away from us, dear Gabrielle?" asked a deep voice at her shoulder.

She started and turned about to see Oliver Seymour smiling down at her, a deep glow in his dark gray eyes. His dark curly hair was dressed carefully à la Byron again today. How handsome he looked! How stunning in his gray silk suit with the flowing golden tie! He wore jade green jewels on his tie, and rings on his hands.

"Good morning, *monsieur*," she said demurely, when she had caught her breath. "Do you also admire this type of art?"

"Immensely," he said, and turned to gaze at the painting. "It reminds me of the ships on which we sailed to the Peninsula."

For some reason, she felt pained at the reminder of the dangers he had endured in the late wars. He had been in some of the worst of the fighting under Wellington, and then later the terrible Battle of Waterloo.

Percy had returned to them, and hovered anxiously. For some reason, he seemed to feel that Minerva did a bad job of masquerading as Gabrielle, and she might

89

be unmasked and denounced at any moment. He glared at Oliver Seymour, who smiled and held out his big, well-formed hand.

"How do you do, Redmond? A splendid morning!"

"Yes, yes, splendid. How do you do?" mumbled Percy, and clasped his hand.

"So you feel able to leave your estates for a time? How fine," said Oliver, who seemed to have some dark motive for speaking so. "I had thought you were absorbed in the spring plowing?"

"I am," said Percy, between his teeth. "But when I heard about Minerva—I mean—and that my cousin had come—"

"Oh, yes, Minerva. How is she? Still feverish?"

"Oh, quite feverish," said "Gabrielle" gaily, then realized her tone was not at all suitable for the illness of a beloved cousin. "I mean—one worries about her, but she is beginning to recover!"

"Oh, splendid. Then may one call upon her?" asked Oliver.

"Oh, no, not now! It is still contagious!" gasped "Gabrielle" and nudged Percy. "Percy was quite worried about her, that is why he came to London!"

"Your devotion does you much credit," said Oliver smoothly. "But you are very close to your sister, I believe."

"Very close," said Percy tautly. "But of course, sometimes she does some foolish stunts, and one is furious with her—"

Oliver looked his question. "Really? Minerva? I thought she was a good, sensible child!"

Minerva punched her brother in his ribs, and he winced. "I mean—getting sick," Percy mumbled.

90

"How is getting sick a foolish stunt?" asked Oliver, persistent as a mosquito.

Percy began to look haunted. What had begun as a veiled rebuke to his sister was turning into a problem. "She was out, looking after some—ah—poor children—yes, children in the slums," he improvised wildly. "And she caught this fever—really too bad of her—"

"This is most interesting. I had not realized that Minerva was doing charity work in the slums. I am surprised her mother permits it, and she an unmarried female of tender years. Do the sights not shock her?" Oliver was leaning on his stick, as though fixed to the spot and too fascinated by the story to move on. Minerva could have shaken him and her brother also.

"First time," gasped Percy, wiping his brow with his handkerchief. "Never again! I assure you!"

Minerva decided to take a firm hand. In gathering horror, she had listened to Percy making up one story after another. She had not realized he had such an imagination! Maybe it ran in the family!

"Of course she will not go again," said Minerva. "It is over and done with, and I am sure she is very sorry she ventured against her mother's wishes. Now, do let us look at the paintings, or the crowds will come in and we shall see nothing!"

She dragged Percy away with her, her fingers pinching his arm violently. To his credit, he did not yelp. He knew he had done wrong! She pointed to the next picture.

"What marvelous use of color!" she said, and nudged Percy.

"Yes, yes, great colors," he said, his gaze fixed on the violent use of reds and scarlet. "What is it?"

"A fire at sea, I should say," said Oliver, strolling after them, and peering at the painting over Minerva's shoulder. She could feel his breath on her cheek, and his warmth just behind her. She edged away; he promptly followed, on pretext of studying the painting more closely.

"I say, look at this one," said Percy anxiously, trying to tug his sister with him.

Oliver by now had her other arm in his, and she felt like a cow at the fair being yanked in two directions. "Look at the fire starting in the hold—I say, that is an explosion of the ammunition," Oliver said, with more genuine interest. "I recall, we had just such a fire at sea, caused by an explosion in the hold where the ammunition was stored. All had to take to small boats—"

Minerva was now torn also between wishing to hear his story, and anxiety over her brother's wish to be gone. Every time Oliver began his few stories of the Peninsular War, she was overcome by some strange and unfamiliar emotions. She felt so—so weak for him, so feverish with anxiety that he had undergone such trials, though they were now over. Whenever she thought of the ordeals of his war experiences, she felt quite cold and shivery, yet hot with fever.

"You had such a bad time of it," she said, in unaccustomed tender tone. "I had no idea how bad it was—war is truly terrible."

"Ah, but you lived in the midst of it in France, my dear Madame Dubois," he said, looking down at her oddly. "Was this not even more dreadful?"

She recalled that she was Gabrielle. "Oh, yes, it was bad. But in the worst of it, I was here in England, with *ma chère tante* and her family," she evaded. "And it was not like being in a battle!"

Percy had deserted her, dropping her arm and going off to see some friend of his at the other side of the room. Oliver said softly, "I like your worry about me. Though of course there is no cause any longer. If only I had known you then—that I might have known the warmth of your anxiety, had the comfort of your letters—"

Someone came behind them to admire the fire at sea. Minerva automatically moved on to the next painting, and gazed at the light sky and billowy clouds behind the headland. "I am sure—you had many letters from ladies to—comfort you," she murmured. "A man—attractive as you are—"

"My mother wrote, and my sister," he said bluntly. "But few ladies cared to try a correspondence which meant long periods of waiting, lost letters, tales of weariness and fatigue, coldness and damp nights. War is mostly waiting miserably for something to happen, and then when it happens it is very bitter. It is not a topic for polite letters. It matters only to those who care deeply."

She gazed up into his eyes, and forgot to be Gabrielle. "I would have cared—deeply," she said. "I could not have been able to help myself."

A light flared in his eyes, he moved more closely, and for a moment she thought he would kiss her lips. "You—would," he whispered. "I thought—so. You have a tender heart, for all your smart appearance, and

93

gay manner. You are a most unusual woman, Madame Dubois!"

They moved on, looked at paintings, but Minerva would have been hard put later on to say what she had seen. She had a vague memory of ships in full sail, green-blue waves, sunsets and sunrises, a blood red sun.

Percy was finished long before the other two, and waited impatiently at the doorway. He grabbed Minerva and pulled her toward their carriage.

"The horses have been standing these two hours," he snapped.

"You are very rude to your cousin," said Oliver sternly. "She was enjoying herself."

Percy bit back angry words, bade him farewell coldly. Minerva was shoved up into the carriage.

As they moved on, Percy said, impassioned, "I cannot go on!"

"Oh, Percy, nonsense!"

"Well, I cannot. I shall trip myself again and again. I cannot stay around Seymour and tell lots more lies. I cannot look him in the face! And Denise Lavery—she has only contempt for me, hanging on the skirts of my widowed cousin!"

Minerva eyed him with worry. "Oh, now, Percy, it is not so bad as that! She is jealous of me, and you will have more of a chance with her! Stick it out, it will be fine, I assure you—"

"I hate telling lies!" muttered Percy gloomily, hanging over the edge of the carriage, and glaring at a high-perch phaeton and its merry driver. "I should be back in Kent, working. Or engaging myself to Denise! Not

94

hanging about art galleries while you make eyes at a fellow I used to respect!"

"What do you mean, 'used to respect'?"

"He is making an ass of himself over you. Everybody was staring at you both!"

"Well—" Minerva could not conceal her delight. "Then it should not be long before he is at my feet! Oh, Percy, just a few more days, I beg you! It won't be long!" she added anxiously.

"I don't think I can endure much more! Denise is mad as fire at me!"

Minerva felt sorry for her honest brother. He was unused to deception, and was not enjoying it as she was. She coaxed, "Just give me a few more days, Percy. I promise you, it shall not be long. I feel that Mr. Seymour is ready to fall at my feet—"

"Then what will you do with him?" he asked perceptively. "Will you kick him? I think not. I think you are liking him rather well these days. But when he finds out you have been deceiving him and making fun of him behind his back, I don't think he'll hang about you any longer! And what then, Minerva Redmond?"

"Well—I don't think that is the case—" she said crossly. She had the picture of her revenge in her mind, and refused to part with it. "He is becoming mad about me, and when he learns I am the same person whom he called dull and dowdy and dour, he will be most upset—"

Percy drooped. "Oh, all right, all right. Minna, it shall be a few more days. But no longer! I shall go mad otherwise!"

"You are a fine brother," she praised him. "You won't be sorry, I promise you."

95

"I'm very sorry already," he muttered, and hopped down as the carriage halted at their door. He helped Minna down, and escorted her into the house.

"I have invited the Laverys to cards on Saturday," she said, hopefully.

"And Denise comes?"

"Her mother wrote, they are all coming."

He perked up a bit at that, but she could see she was going to have a time with him. He was turning stubborn. She must work faster, and get Oliver Seymour to her feet more quickly!

Chapter 7

OLIVER SEYMOUR sat at his huge rosewood desk, and rolled his jade pen around in his large fingers. He frowned absently at the large bookshelves that lined the walls.

The words formed in his mind, but before them rose the picture of an alluring oval face, sparkling green, mischievous eyes, thick masses of silky red-gold curls— He groaned, and dipped his pen in the ink.

He drew a sheet of creamy notepaper to him, and began to write.

Dearest Mother,

    I hope this finds you well, and also my dearest sister. My thoughts are often with you and with her. Your letters of her condition are most reassuring. I hope to see the new little one before long.

    This letter comes to you to beg your presence in London. A most intriguing situation is forming, and I wish you to come with haste and aid me.

    You may find it hard to credit, as I do. But I feel that young Minerva Redmond is playing a little game with me, and with all London. I can scarce credit it myself, but she is I think masquerading as her own French cousin!

Oliver laid down the pen to think, a smile around his mouth. His eyes shone as he thought of the latest exchange of dialogue with the intriguing Madame Dubois. Then he picked up the pen and continued.

Imagine, if you will, a beautiful French widow of some twenty-five years, with beautiful green eyes, masses of red-gold hair, who refuses to wear black or even gray for her late 'beloved' husband. Imagine a delectable madame who exchanges most flirtatious comments with me, as she dances exquisite waltzes. I found myself madly intrigued by her, and convinced she was a sad flirt, who might yet make a pretty mistress! Oh, I know you gasp, but such was my state of mind! She is quick of tongue, warm of passion in her kisses, yet refused to come alone to my house.

However, at the same time, young Minerva Redmond has disappeared into her bedroom, with fever and some illness which has not yet been fully described to me. She has never been seen in the same room with Madame Dubois! After some two weeks of devotion to the French lady, I am becoming suspicious. The French accent slips, the French lady reveals some knowledge of England she could not easily know, and her brother Percy came to London to escort her about. Yet he shows more impatience with her than devotion.

Oliver drew in his lip, frowned over his letter.

I mean, Minerva's brother Percy came. Forgive my incoherence. I am quite bewildered, confused, and puzzled.

At any rate, this day finds me set upon solving the puzzle. If she is truly Madame Dubois, a French widow, then that is one matter. However, if she is young Minerva Redmond, set upon mischief, and dangling me on a string, that is quite another matter! I think you will be intrigued by the sight of your son dangling helplessly to the play of a young puppet-master!

98

I send you Hendricks, the barouche, and two carriages for your trunks, and my fond hopes that you will soon consent to attend me in London. I warrant you will have a splendid time of it. You wish me to marry soon. Well, I may think of doing so, should the puzzle end as I wish it to do! But what is the lady? Widow of some five years? Or girl playing a part with wicked accuracy, and showing much more depth than I had dreamed in her? Come soon, and discover for yourself!

Your loving son, Oliver.

He read over the letter, sanded it, and folded it, then rang for Hendricks. The coachman, old and faithful in the Seymour service, promised to carry out Oliver's wishes to the line, and soon departed with carriages and outriders.

Oliver then looked at the gold ormolu clock on the wall of the study. Ten o'clock. He returned to his bedroom, and removed his gold lounging robe, and his valet held out the fine silk waistcoat of gold and silver thread.

Oliver put it on, patted it down, then donned the blue silk jacket the valet held for him. The valet smoothed down the back devotedly, until not a wrinkle showed on his master's muscular back. Oliver eyed himself anxiously in the mirror. He had always cared about appearance; it was the mark of the gentleman, whether one wore trim uniform or London town clothes, or country styles. But never had he felt so keen to look well. Madame Dubois always noticed, and sometimes commented, and he did not want to be outshone by any French dandy.

Was she truly Minerva Redmond? He could scarce believe it himself, yet clues had started to show, now that he was on the lookout for them. When he had first

99

guessed, he scarcely knew. Yet the continued absence of Minerva disturbed him. His little mousy friend was a fine girl, though dull, and prim. If she were truly so ill, he was very sorry. Yet—yet the eyes were the same, the same shade of green, their faces had the same oval—and the same color hair, though it looked so different.

Yet—people said Gabrielle Mably had been of the same coloring as Minerva Redmond, when they were girls together in Kent. He might be wrong!

What if the lady who made him quiver with passion, who caused his heart to beat twice as rapidly, was really a widow? What would he feel then? Married five years, with no children! Married to an elderly Frenchman—for his money? Why else? It showed a want of romantic feeling that disturbed him. And the fact that she had no children might mean a lack in her husband—or a lack in herself!

And Oliver Seymour owed it to his family and his estates, his lineage, to have a son to follow him! And he did want children. He enjoyed them, he longed for his own sons and daughters, to complete his life.

A wife would be all very well, but one must marry well, and with circumspection, with due regard to what one owed to the family.

He set jade cufflinks into his wrists, and the valet fastened them, and the jade stud in his blue tie. The pale green jade was set off by the electric blue of his suit. He surveyed himself with satisfaction.

"*Very* handsome, sir, if I may say so," murmured the valet. He brushed an imaginary fleck from the collar, and stood back critically. He seemed to sense that his
100

master went a-courting. "You will return for luncheon, sir?"

"Er, probably. About one o'clock, if all goes well."

"May I wish you well, sir," said the valet fervently.

"You may. Thank you," and Oliver strode out eagerly to seek his fate.

He stepped into his carriage and directed the man, though it was scarcely necessary. Even the horses must know the way by now to the Redmond townhouse.

By eleven o'clock, he was stepping down and striding to the door. The butler swung open the door soundlessly, and greeted him.

"The ladies and Mr. Percival are in the drawing room, Mr. Seymour," he said, and swung open that door with a flourish.

Oliver was delighted to find he was early, and nobody else had come yet. He kissed the hand of Mrs. Redmond, then of the languid Madame Dubois, then shook the hand of Percival.

Then he seated himself opposite to Madame Dubois, and admired the sight of her, lounging on a chaise longue, her dainty feet in golden slippers on the foot of it, her lovely slim rounded form attired in a gown of daffodil yellow, the white lace at her throat revealing something of the white breasts they only half concealed. She must be a widow, he thought, involuntarily. No virginal girl would dare wear that gown—and yet— He looked at her hands. No rings! And no marks of rings! She wore only a golden bracelet on her left wrist.

"You are well today?" he asked, conventionally.

Her smile dazzled, her eyes provoked. "Very well.

101

And you, *monsieur,* there are marks under your eyes? You have not slept?"

She picked up a lace fan and surveyed him over it. Her green eyes sparkled.

"My dreams keep me awake, *madame!*"

"How odd!" she remarked, with a little low giggle that was pure delight to his ears. "Your dreams—keep you awake? Explain if you will, *monsieur!*"

"Oh, I have begun to dream great dreams, Madame Dubois! Worlds to conquer, conquests to make! From the hot sun of the equator—" And he looked significantly at her wildly curling red-gold hair, down over her body. "Down to the belt of Orion, and to the delights of the tropics—to the Cape of Good Hope—"

Percy strolled over to them. "I say, that is all rank nonsense," he said, bewildered. "You have your geography all wrong, Seymour! If you don't mind, I shall obtain an atlas—"

"Gabrielle" burst out laughing, her cheeks very pink. "He teases, Percival!" she said in her pretty drawl. "He thinks to confuse me, knowing I do not—know geography!"

"Oh, is that it?" muttered Percy. "I swear, nobody knows what you two talk about! At the art gallery, Mother, they talked of fires at sea, and all that nonsense. All I saw were splashes of red paint."

"Much is in the eye of the beholder," said Oliver, and looked again boldly over his tempting mistress. When he was with her, he found it difficult to think, he could only feel, his pulses boiling, his heart pounding, his breathing quickened. And he longed only to pull her into his arms, her body over his ruthless arm, as he punished her softly with kisses.

102

The butler opened the door, a maid wheeled in the silver tea tray, and Mrs. Redmond seated herself to pour. Minerva or Gabrielle, whichever she was, made no move to help. Perhaps she was the visiting French cousin; surely otherwise she would jump up to take around plates—Minerva always had, as he recalled. Minerva had been a good, eager, obedient girl, except sometimes sullen of temper, and quick of biting tongue.

He looked at the little red tongue of Gabrielle, licking quickly at a cake crumb, and tempting him with the sight, recalling the feel of it in his mouth when she had responded to his kiss. Oh, if he but might have the right to crush her to him, to press his mouth to hers, to thrust his tongue into that little pink kitten-mouth, to lick the pearllike teeth, to touch that red tongue—

"Don't you care for your tea with cream?" murmured Mrs. Redmond.

Oliver started. "Oh, yes, fine, fine."

He caught the keen look of the lady. Could she really join in such a rash escapade, to deceive him and all London? She was such a practical, sensible, placid lady. Oh, no, his imagination had run riot! He must be wrong. He sipped, thoughtfully, and formed the questions he had determined to ask.

"Ah—how is Minerva today?"

"Fine," said "Gabrielle" with a smile.

"Fine!" he exclaimed. "She is well again?"

"Oh, no, not well!" cried Gabrielle. "I mean—she is so much better! She is practically well!"

"Practically well!" echoed Percy, eating a cake in one bite.

"And the fever?" he asked, looking about as though

to see Minerva enter the room. "She joins us today, the fever is gone?"

"Oh, no, no," said Gabrielle quickly. "The fever is gone, but she is not well, yet, I mean—"

He dashed in ruthlessly, while she still seemed confused. "I never did comprehend, what is the exact nature of her illness?"

"Fever," said Gabrielle, nodding her pretty head wisely. "A very—severe—fever."

"But a fever has many causes," he said. "One can have a fever from a bullet wound, or a disease, or a grippe—"

"Ah—well, the fever was—" And Gabrielle looked helplessly toward Mrs. Redmond. *"Tante,* the name of it—"

"Chicken pox," said Mrs. Redmond crisply. "Yes, it was chicken pox."

"Ah, very serious, then, to last so long? Almost three weeks," said Oliver thoughtfully, thinking frantically what little he knew about chicken pox. "Is that like smallpox? You have been quarantined?"

"No, no," said Mrs. Redmond, smiling. "It is usually a disease of childhood, but dear Minerva did not have it then. She caught it from some children—"

"Ah, yes, as she visited in some slums," said Oliver, nodding.

"Slums!" gasped Mrs. Redmond. "Oh, never—"

"Yes, I have confessed to him," said Gabrielle quickly. "Dear foolish Minerva visited the slums, and got the—ah—pox—from some children—"

To Oliver's keen eye, Mrs. Redmond was a moment in recovering. But she had a bland face, he could not be completely sure she had been taken by surprise.

"Chicken pox," said Mrs. Redmond. "Do not make it worse than it is," she added sharply. "If it had been smallpox, we would not all be so casually sitting here! We should all be in quarantine, and confined to a doctor's care!"

"Not a bad idea," muttered Percy gloomily.

"Nonsense," said Gabrielle heartily. She gave Oliver a delicious wink, and murmured so only he could hear, "He finds his courtship of—you know who—goes heavily!"

He bent devotedly closer. "Do you encourage that—courtship?"

"Of course! I wish to see him happy, and she is a sweet girl," said Gabrielle, with no trace of accent.

"Hum. I thought he escorted you about with great devotion."

"He is a devoted cousin, he always was," sighed Gabrielle, with a return of accent. "Zis is why my visits to England were always so—enjoyable! My dearest cousins—zey are so sweet to me—"

Yes, her accent did come and go, his eyes and ears were noting. She had a little way of pursing up her lips when she spoke in a Frenchy way. Now that he was alert to it, he could tell when she was putting on the accent. The little demon, he thought. He was practically certain that she was really Minerva! But how to be sure?

"Well, one hopes that dear little Minerva will be completely well before long," he said jovially, watching Gabrielle's face alertly. "She is very intelligent, is she not? She puts much value on books, so you said, rather than people."

"Oh, Minerva likes people!" said Gabrielle quickly,

105

with a glance at Mrs. Redmond. "It is just that she is—shy. Verree shy, dear little girl! One must bring her out more!"

"Yes, I must bring her out more," said Mrs. Redmond thoughtfully. "I have not pushed her enough, I fear. She dances well, but sits in corners. I cannot have that any longer! When she is well again, we shall see to it, eh, Gabrielle?" And she exchanged a stern look with her "niece."

"But of course!" cried Gabrielle, showing her small pearly teeth. "She shall come out of her shell! I zink she shall wear more bright clothes too! I talked to her about zis—"

"You talked to her—while she is in isolation?" asked Oliver quickly.

"Through the open door." Gabrielle smiled. "One may now speak to her in zis way—"

Oliver stood up. "Oh, then let me go upstairs and speak to her! She must be very dull, to be alone so much! I shall just give her my good wishes for her recovery—"

All three sprang to their feet to stop him.

"No, no, you cannot go up there!" cried Percy, standing before the closed drawing room door with outspread arms. He looked very alarmed.

"Of course not!" gasped Gabrielle, her hand outstretched in appeal. "Pray, dear Oliver, come back and sit down—"

"Why cannot I speak to her? I have known her for years, she will be glad to have a friend, I should think," said Oliver, with sweet reasonableness. "Alone all these weeks, poor little child—"

"She is not a little child!" said Gabrielle between her teeth. One might say, she snapped.

Mrs. Redmond said, "She is not dressed, Oliver, she is in nightclothes. It would not be proper. Do come and sit down. All of you! Sit down!"

She prevailed. Gabrielle sank onto the chaise longue once more, looking rather pale. Percy sat down on the edge of a straight chair near the door. Mrs. Redmond sat at the tea tray and asked, "More tea, anyone? Another almond cookie, anyone?"

No one seemed hungry or thirsty. Gabrielle stretched out, and surveyed her slippers absently. Oliver's gaze went hungrily over the slim form in the yellow gown; it showed the lines of her figure in a manner that made him burn! Surely, her mother would not allow Minerva to wear such a gown— Yet he could remember when his sister Eleanor was being courted, she had worn some extreme gowns, to their father's keen displeasure. And his mother had upheld her, for some strange reason, though she had been overprotective of Eleanor's virtues for years. Must be something about it, mused Oliver. When a girl was intent on matrimony, perhaps more license was permitted—it certainly did make a fellow more keen!

"Well, I must be on my way. A fellow has some jade he is thinking of selling," said Oliver, rising. "I want to be in on the bidding of it this morning."

"Oh, really? You have such lovely jade, and such a large collection, I should not think you long for more." Gabrielle sat up languidly, and permitted him to take her hand.

"There is something about jade," said Oliver with a smile. He brushed back the loose sleeve, and with his back to Mrs. Redmond and Percy, he bent to kiss her hand. Only he kissed the wrist instead, with a long lingering kiss, then opened her hand, and pressed a kiss into her palm.

"S-something about j-jade," stammered Gabrielle. "What—d-do you mean?"

"It intrigues one. The more one has, the more one wants," said Oliver, his eyes significantly focused on her red lips. "One—hungers for more. I think to add some French jade to my collection."

"Really?" said Percy, with some slight interest. "I have heard of Chinese jade, and other Oriental pieces—but never from France. Do they mine it there?"

"They—form it in France," said Oliver with a smile. There was some pink color in Gabrielle's cheeks, he was happy to see. She had his message! "So I must hasten to acquire the French jade. It may be snatched up by some other fellow!"

"Yes, one must take care, not to be too rash and foolish," said Gabrielle, lazily, leaning back, her eyes half closed. "When one is too confident, one sometimes loses all!"

"I shall be careful, you may be sure," he said, and took his departure, well satisfied.

Chapter 8

SEVERAL DAYS later, Oliver Seymour sent word to Mrs. Redmond, Percival, and Madame Dubois that his mother had come to London to stay with him:

"Mother has expressed a wish to visit Vauxhall Gardens. There is some female singer who is performing tonight. May I hope for your company to attend with us? It looks to be a fine evening for early May."

Minerva was transported. She adored Vauxhall though she had not gone often. "Is it masquerade night?" she cried eagerly.

"I certainly hope not!" said Percy repressively. "All would be rowdy and disagreeable."

"Oliver would not suggest it if it was masquerade night, I feel sure," added Betsy Redmond. They looked in the latest gazette, and sure enough it was a regular night, not masquerade.

"I should think," said Percy, "that you have enough of masquerade, dearest sister!"

"Well, I enjoy it tremendously." Minerva smiled, making a little face at him.

"I do not!" he said distinctly. "Denise is furious with me, and I thought she was going to refuse to dance with me the other night. I have a sad reputation with her, you may be sure! Dangling about my cousin's skirts!"

"All will come well, Percy," soothed Minerva. "She

is sure to come about when your cousin goes back to France!"

"I can scarcely wait!" he muttered. He sighed deeply, and Minerva gazed at him anxiously. Percy was more and more impatient and down in the mouth.

"Well, it will all work out," said Betsy Redmond. She asked Minerva what she would wear that evening, and the talk turned to clothes.

Minerva finally wore her daring gold tissue silk gown, which clung tightly all down her. She wore over it a black velvet cloak of her mother's, and her hair was a blaze of curls and tendrils, with golden hairpins, and the jade butterfly in it.

Oliver was enchanted with her, when he saw her. He and his mother had come early with the large comfortable barouche, and soon they were on their way to the Gardens.

Mrs. Anthony Seymour was a tall, stately, elegant woman. She had lost her husband some years ago, and now wore black or dark gray all the time, but she was not a stifling personality. She had a keen sense of humor like her son's, thought Minerva, when the lady commented with mock gravity on the costumes of persons at Vauxhall.

"I thought it was not masquerade night, Oliver!" she exclaimed, as one clown in gaudy garments ran past them as they strolled to their supper box. "That cannot be a costume of fashionable London!"

"No, Mother, we have not gone so far!" he reassured her with a laugh. "I warrant the way styles go, we may be wearing patches and gauds before long, but so far— no. But you will be amused by the pantomime tonight,

110

it is a version of Punch and Judy by persons singing the parts. I have heard it is vastly amusing."

"So you have been here before this spring?" asked Minerva demurely, glancing up at him sideways.

"No, *madame*, I have not! A friend has, and recommended it."

"I warrant you come often—perhaps on masquerade night?"

He said in her ear, "I am not the one fond of masquerades! Though I could become so!"

She had been idly teasing him when he said that. A gasp broke from her lips. Could he mean—had he guessed?—but no! He could not know she was masquerading as her cousin. Or could he? No, he said nothing, he knew nothing!

All the more frantically, she flirted with him. He must not guess that she was Minerva! Not until she was ready!

He seated them devotedly in one of the finest boxes, a large, elegant one with golden curtains, and a splendid view of the stage. Someone was singing. Minerva propped her elbows on the table, and listened with keen enjoyment. The lady was singing some melodies from a current popular theater piece, and her voice rang out in the tree-filled Gardens. Flowers dotted the grounds, in glorious plots of colors of spring, pinks and blues and pale yellows.

"Are there fireworks tonight?" asked Percy, sounding happier.

"Yes, there are," said Oliver. "I asked especially."

"Oh, splendid," he said. "I do like that."

"And do you, *madame?*" asked Oliver, leaning to

111

Minerva, and managing to kiss her ear lobe as he did so. A thrill went down her spine.

"Oh, yes, immensely," she said dreamily. "Lots of color and excitement, and beauty."

"Our tastes match exactly." He smiled, looking significantly down over her, as much as he could see at the table.

The Gardens looked especially lovely that night, even more beautiful than when Minerva had come in past years. The Japanese lanterns glowed in the trees and on poles, shining lights in the colored papers of pink and gold, blue and green, purple and wine. They swayed in the wind, and the lights fluttered like fireflies.

The music was like golden light as a flutist played a solo with the orchestra. They listened, enchanted, as the music wove a magic line into the colorful evening.

"Marvelous," murmured Katherine Seymour. "I remember well an evening I came here with dearest Anthony—"

"And I with my Arnold," sighed Betsy Redmond.

A shiver went down Minerva. Would she come here one night, widowed and alone, and remembering past glories? How short was life, how brief, like a candle that blew out in the wind.

"What are you thinking?" whispered Oliver.

"How short is life," she said, in a melancholy voice. "How brief—a candle is not longer. Then one lives with memories."

"Yes, so one must make the memories so beautiful, that they light up one's life hereafter. Don't you think so? One must seize the moment, and be happy in it.

Love and laugh, give of one's self, enjoy the passions of the moment—"

Minerva turned from her contemplation of the stage, to gaze deeply into the gray eyes. Was he serious, or teasing? Mischievous, or somber as she felt for the moment? She saw no amusement in his eyes, but she did see a light of passion.

For a moment, her purpose was jolted. What if she failed? What if "Gabrielle" must return to France, for Oliver wanted only a mistress, and lived as lightly as he spoke? How horrid that would be!

"Oh, Madame Haswell will sing now!" cried Katherine Seymour joyously. "Oh, I remember when she sang years ago—I wonder if her voice is as splendid?"

They all hushed as the beautiful opera singer came out on the stage. She was attired in a brilliant green and silver gown with a train that trailed behind her a full six feet, and sparkled and shimmered in the lantern lights.

"Like a peacock's tail," whispered Oliver. "Look how it shines—"

She did look like a peacock, all glimmering and shining, thought Minerva as she nodded.

"Let us hope she does not sing as one!" he muttered in her ear, wickedly. "They have a very scream!"

She giggled, unable to control herself, and her mother frowned at her. She suppressed the laugh with an intense effort. What a tease Oliver was! He knew she found it hard not to laugh aloud!

Madame Haswell sang much better than they had hoped. She sang first several arias, then later returned and in another even more gorgeous gown she sang with a choral group some magnificent opera numbers, with

113

the orchestra banging away with great enthusiasm at their drums and all. It was quite a splendid evening, and earned fine praise in the gazettes that week.

Minerva listened in a daze. Oliver hung at her elbow and kept whispering in her ear—not to disturb her, but to comment, point out things, tell her about some singer or player. And every so often his lips touched her ear, or her cheek, and sent another wild thrill down her. He managed to hold her elbow, her arm, or even her hand, and played with her fingers, under cover of the darkness in the box.

She was not sure her mother did not notice. And Mrs. Seymour had keen eyesight, but none said anything. Perhaps she would hear about this later! But for now she did not care. She had rarely felt so excited, so thrilled, so moved. Both by the singing and the music, and by Oliver!

When the interlude came, the waiters came scurrying with their dinner. They had many people to serve so quickly, and she marveled how they brought the chilled wines, and opened them, served the glasses. Another swarm of waiters brought the plates of cold beef and mustard, the chunks of boiled lamb and mint sauce, bowls of fresh fruit chopped and swimming in a delicious coconut cordial. Desserts were custards, syllabubs laced with wine, and platters of beautiful pastries.

Oliver teased Minerva by putting little bits of food between her lips, feeding her with his fork, causing her to drink from one glass, then he would take the glass and drink from the same place.

Mrs. Redmond was chattering with Mrs. Seymour, and managed to keep Percy's attention from them most
114

of the time. Minerva sat in the corner of the box, with Oliver's attentions making her feel very hot and bothered, and wished the night would never end!

Leaving the wines on the table, and the pastries, the waiters picked up the plates and the leavings, and scurried away just in time for the next part of the program. The stage had been cleared, many had pounded vigorously with hammers and tools, and now the curtains opened. There was a ship in full sail and what looked like an ocean! The audience oohed and ahhed and clapped vigorously.

The scene turned out to be a battle at sea. While Minerva marveled, and Oliver chuckled so hard he almost fell over, the ships bravely rolled across the oceans at each other, fired their broadsides to the vigorously playing orchestra. Fireworks filled the air, supposedly from the cannons. Lighting resembling lightning sparkled in the air; thunder rumbled, courtesy of drums. Then the masterpiece. Majestically one ship turned tail up, and sank slowly into the water!

Oliver rocked with laughter, howling with mirth. Percy joined him reluctantly.

"I say, it is funny," said Percy, "but how do they do it?"

"I don't know," gasped Oliver. "But I never saw anything so funny in my days! They should see a real fight at sea! God, it is a howl! Those pretty little ships passing and passing! Oh, my God—"

"Oliver, darling, I pray you, do not swear before us," begged his mother plaintively. "I know it is funny—"

"Forgive me, ladies. I am so sorry!" He apologized

115

at once, wiping his eyes with his handkerchief. "Forgot myself! You must excuse me—terribly sorry!"

He was forgiven at once. Minerva looked at him reproachfully. "I thought it looked very real and frightening, Oliver! How can you laugh so?"

He patted her hand, managing to curl his big fingers around hers intimately. "My dear, if one did not laugh, one would cry! I have seen real battles, men with big holes blown in them, and blood flowing everywhere. And to think they now make it an amusement for a half-drunken mob! It is so ironic, I have to laugh! Battles, all prettied up! God, how crazy is Thy world!"

He spoke in a low savage tone, the others did not hear him. Impulsively, Minerva squeezed his fingers, her other hand on their joined hands.

"I am sorry, I did not understand," she said in a soft voice. "You must be torn between mirth and anguish, to see such a sight after all your battles. Yes, how can they treat a battle of war as an amusement in the Gardens? Will they next show us wounded and dying men, as an entertainment?"

"You do understand," he said intensely. "Oh—Gabrielle—what it is to have someone to know one's mind, to comprehend one's feelings—I want you to know—"

"Dear me, I feel so full," yawned Percy, as the curtain went down and the chatter rose up again. "I think I shall take a stroll!"

"Yes, do that," agreed Oliver with a sudden change of tone, so amiable and nice. "I'll take Minerva around to see the lights and the flowers. Why don't you take Mother and Mrs. Redmond the other way?"

He got up so quickly, they had no time to protest.

He brought Minerva up with him, and they went off into the darkness alone.

He was so fast, she could only gasp. "Really, Oliver, we should remain with Mother—I don't know what they will say—"

She faltered. She had said "Mother"—had he noticed?

He said nothing, only rushing her into the dark path near their box. She said, as though repeating,

"Really, Oliver, we should remain with *your* mother—and my aunt—and Percival! I think we should be together—"

"And I have looked forward to having you alone!" he said, with a laugh in his voice. "Come along, Gabrielle! I don't want to drag you!"

They had lost the others. She looked back over her shoulder. Crowds swarmed in the paths, leaving their boxes, talking, chattering, laughing, exclaiming. One girl shrieked, a man's laugh echoed. Minerva drew closer to Oliver. It seemed that on the dark paths of Vauxhall Gardens, all kinds of things went on!

"That's right, stick to me," said Oliver cheerily, putting his arm possessively about her waist. "I say, look at the lights! They are very pretty tonight!"

She looked at the little lights, now flaring up before them to light the dark trees and walks. They were enchantingly lovely, all the light colors of the rainbows flaring in the night. They strolled along, his arm about her, to keep her from the young gallants who would knowingly jostle her, and they admired the cascades, the fountains, the statues, the little boxes of fine company. All London-town seemed to have turned out that

117

fine night, dressed in beautiful finery, to admire and be admired.

Then Oliver turned into one particularly dark path, near some trees lined with lanterns, and pushe.. ner into the shadow of some tall bushes. Minerva said, "What are—"

Oliver's mouth closed over hers, and his arms pulled her so close she could scarcely breathe. Her hands went to his shoulders, involuntarily. She thought she would fall over backward, he was pushing her back over his arm. The only way to keep her balance was to cling to his hard shoulders, and her fingers bit into his arms.

His mouth was warm and eager. Her lips were parted, and his mouth was moving over her lips in nibbling, biting kisses. She felt half faint with the pleasure of it. Something warm was rising inside her, from her thighs to her throat, something like an emotional wave of excitement, like that caused by some very sentimental music—only different.

She could hear the orchestra in the distance, the light-music one this time, and the faint waltz tune seemed to melt her into a rhythm of love. Oliver's mouth was moving on hers, back and forth, stroking her lips in the most sensuous kiss she had ever felt. His tongue was pressed into her mouth, thrusting back and forth against her teeth and tongue, and the slow erotic movement of his mouth was like a little waltz.

Her brain was dizzy. All that wine, she thought. Oliver had kept plying her with wine—on purpose? But she could not think straight. All she could do was feel.

And she felt his hands on her silky back, moving up and down from her thighs to her waist up behind her

118

back—and down again. His hands, so hard and pulling her to him—his fingers probing as though he played an instrument on her spine. When he touched her thighs again, he pulled, and she felt the hard masculine throb of his thighs, like something moving and growing there.

She thought dimly of her mother's lectures, demurely delivered, on the subject of Men and Marriage. Oh, dear, but she was not Married! Yet—here was a Man. Very much a Man. Very masculine, and demanding—and the lectures—what had her mother said? It was hard to remember.

Something about—when one's husband demanded, one submitted. A female was made to surrender and do as her husband wished.

But what happened when he demanded—and he was not her husband? Minerva groaned a little in her throat, he was pressing her so tightly to his body, her back was bent, and she could not stand upright, and his face was pressed to her warm bare throat, and his lips were on her breast, moving hungrily down it to the nipple— How had he gotten her dress open, it was buttoned to the throat?

But she could not think clearly at all. Some time, his fingers had moved among the little buttons, and now she was naked to the breast, below them—and his tongue licked on the nipple, and she moaned with the taut excitement.

"I must—have you," he muttered. "I must—oh, God—"

He was swearing again, his mother would not approve— Oh, his mother! And her mother! Minerva pressed back against the tree trunk, and tried to push his hard shoulders.

"Oliver—please—I pray you—Oliver!" She evaded, and twisted and squirmed, but it seemed to make him the more ardent. His mouth returned to her lips, and he pressed against them so hard he hurt her. And something hot boiled in her, and made her weak and trembling. He was shaking against her, she felt him tremble—what was the matter with him?

"Oliver—I pray you—" She tried again when his mouth moved to her white shoulder, and down again to the bared breast. "Oliver—stop! Stop!"

He finally lifted his head, and stared down at her in the darkness. She was shaking, her eyes huge in the dim light. "Oh, God, what am I doing?" he muttered.

"You must—stop—we must—go back—your mother, Oliver!" She faltered, trying to think of words to persuade him.

"You are so sweet! Kiss me again!"

He pulled her tight again, but she had managed to get one arm between them. "Please—you are hurting me!"

At the little cry, he paused again. He groaned. "I am—hurting you—truly?"

"Yes—my arm—pray, Oliver, you must—s-stop!"

He bent his head, and put his face against her throat. She thought he would tear at her again, and kiss her all over, then she realized he was standing very still, breathing deeply. Finally he lifted his head.

"Yes—I am sorry—" he said hoarsely, in an unnatural voice. "We must—go back—yes, of course—" He drew back, and looked down at her, then his hands left her back, and he put them on the little buttons, and began to fasten them slowly.

She stood still, and let him fasten them all up again, right to her throat. She was breathing unsteadily, her mouth was on fire, her body was so hot she felt as though she had a violent fever, in spite of the cool breeze sweeping through the Gardens from the river.

And she had wanted him to go on kissing her! What was wrong with her?

He took her arm, and they began to stroll back to the main section where their box was. They could hear the orchestra tuning up, it was time for the next part. She knew her hair was mussed wildly, she tried to pat back some of the curls.

"May I call upon you tomorrow?" he asked, as they came near the box. His voice was thick.

"Yes—" she whispered. "Oh—not in the morning. Mama will sleep late—"

She did not even know what she said. He did not seem to notice either.

"Then in the afternoon—about three o'clock?"

Was he going to propose? Her heart was beating in great uneven thumps. Oh, how she wanted him to propose! She would say yes—she was madly in love with him—he was so exciting, so fine, so handsome, so marvelous— But first!

First, she would unmask, and declaim how stupid he had been to think her dull and dowdy. He must grovel at her feet! She must have her revenge, she must!

And tomorrow would be the day!

"Tomorrow—at three—" she whispered, and he helped her up into the box. She sat down at the table.

121

The others looked at them curiously.

"You were gone a long time," said Mrs. Redmond, in a rather chilly manner. "Did you get lost?"

"I am sorry, yes," said Oliver. "The paths are rather a maze, didn't you find them so?"

"No, I had no trouble," said Percy, definitely. "But of course I was with my mother and Mrs. Seymour!"

Poor Oliver looked discomposed for once! Minerva hastened to his rescue.

"We were not gone long," she said quickly. "Look, the next part is just starting. There goes the curtain—oh, I do hope the lady will sing again!"

She did sing again, to Minerva's relief. The sweet singing, the bright costumes all distracted them, and left a pleasant taste. Then the conclusion was a marvelous brilliant display of fireworks, which popped and boomed and shot into the air in a most satisfactory manner.

In the thrilling finale, Oliver sought Minerva's hand, and held it in his under the table, and squeezed her fingers so hard it hurt. But she did not mind, it was part of the purple night, the starry fireworks, the laughter and singing and joy. And he loved her, she was sure of it. And tomorrow—tomorrow—the masks would come off, and she would have her revenge—and then accept him!

Oh, life was marvelous! She smiled up at the last gaudy lights, the flags and stars and spangles lighting up the skies over London. And she pressed Oliver's fingers secretly, to encourage him. Tomorrow! Tomorrow! Tomorrow!

Chapter 9

MINERVA COULD scarcely sleep that night. Her heart thumped; she kept waking, to stare into the darkness, and remember the way Oliver had held her, kissed her, run his hands over her.

Oh, how she shivered at the remembrance!

Perhaps, tomorrow night they would be engaged! And he would have the right to kiss her, and hold her—and one day soon they would marry—and then—oh!

She squirmed in the wide bed, and smiled at nothing. Marriage, the unknown mystery—she knew little about it, because people did not talk much. But women whispered, and maids giggled, and she knew married people shared a bedroom, and pretty soon the woman had a child, a baby—

Oliver's child! It would be delightful. He was nice with children, he had spoken affectionately last night about his sister's brood. He would make a fine father! And oh, she longed to be a married lady, with a husband like Oliver to be attentive, and helpful—and to hold her the way he had, only closer!

She liked his townhouse, it was large and splendid, but even more it was warm and comfortable. It spoke of quiet good taste, excellent furniture, carpets, porcelain. And Oliver's jade collection! And Oliver—teasing, loving, possessive, his gray eyes alight! He would be fun to be married to, she thought contentedly.

The estates in the country, they would be near her own family in Kent. They would visit back and forth, and not be strangers. She looked forward to coming to know his sister Eleanor and her family better.

She slept, wakened, slept again. Jessie did not come to her to snap open the curtains and speak in a cheerful, brutal manner about how late she was. Nobody came.

Miverva blinked at the gray light in the room. Finally she rose and opened the curtains, then barefoot crossed to the door and opened it. She listened. Had she heard a carriage? What time was it? What was going on?

Then she heard a laugh, and her blood went cold. Literally. She turned chill, and shivered there in the hallway, in her nightrail, one foot over the other against the cold of the hall floor. That laugh!

She had heard it often as a teenager, peering down the stairs to watch the older people as they came for an evening to which she was not invited. It echoed from the drawing room as the others entertained at tea. It mocked her as she blushed redly from mingled shyness and fury. That laugh!

Jessie came along the hallway carrying a pitcher of hot water. "Awake, are ye?" she asked grimly.

"Is—Gabrielle—here? In London? Here, in the house?"

"Aye, that she is! Come along now, you're late. You'll wash and dress and come down to breakfast."

Minerva walked slowly back into her bedroom, her heart down in her bare feet. She submitted to washing and dressing.

"When—did she come?"

"On the night ship, then the train from Dover this
124

morning. Come with a beau, she did. He looks like a monkey. He's a lawyer, but smart enough, I'll warrant! She looks about ten years older than you, and she always was twenty years smarter. You'll have to look to yourself, Miss Minerva!" said Jessie, ominously.

Minerva knew that. Dully, she knew that. Gabrielle had come, and it would ruin everything.

"But why—why now?"

"Your mother sent for her," said Jessie, bluntly. And Minerva thought her heart would break in two.

"Mother did?" It was betrayal, it was bitter gall.

"Aye. Wanted to put an end to your masquerade, and I don't blame her. A fine pickle you are in, to be sure!"

"It would have been all right—" Today, it would have ended, she thought, as she slipped into the blue muslin gown that Jessie held for her.

"This dress?" asked Minerva as the maid began to fasten it. "I thought to wear my yellow silk—"

"You'll be going back to being Miss Minerva again, I'll warrant!"

"But I love my new gowns—"

"There can't be two Madame Duboises in the house!"

"No. I suppose not."

"And your mother sent a note to Mr. Oliver, saying not to come today, as you have a guest from France."

Miverva jerked. "Oh, she cannot!" she gasped. "Oliver comes to see me—and he would guess—oh, she cannot—"

"Yes, she can. Got to straighten out matters with your cousin, and get it all set, before Mr. Oliver comes again. And the guest from France, that's Madame Dubois's beau, Mr. Claudel."

Minerva's life had shattered into small pieces, quite

125

incapable of mending. Dully she went down to breakfast in the smaller dining room, to find her French cousin chattering gaily.

A strange man sprang up, but Minerva scarcely noted him at first. Her gaze was on her cousin. Madame Gabrielle Mably Dubois, herself, to the life. One inch taller, of Minerva's build, but slightly larger in the bust and thighs. Rounded, mature, wise, her green eyes keen and shrewd.

"*Chère* Minerva!" cried Gabrielle, embracing her, and pressing a perfumed kiss on either cheek. "Just the same as ever!"

It was a blow below Minna's waist, and she flinched, and held out her hand to the man.

He was a surprise. She had thought he would be a smart French dandy, tall and uniformed, perhaps. Instead, her gaze met that of a slightly built man, of some thirty-five years. His face was lined and wrinkled like that of a clever monkey, and his cheeks were scarred. He wore a neat gray suit, and a ruffled white shirt. But he sagged in it, his shoulders were bent, as though from years of hardship. And his brown eyes were sadly wise, like those of a monkey in the zoological gardens Minerva had seen as a child.

"François Claudel," Gabrielle introduced him. "My lawyer. And dearest best friend." And she patted his slim arm.

"So happy to meet you," he murmured in accented English. He bowed from the waist, and brought Minerva's hand just to his lips, but did not touch them. He straightened, and looked at her keenly, as though through her.

"They were just telling us about the war," said Percy
126

excitedly, as all were seated again. "They lived through the most awful times!"

"But, Gabrielle, you were with us in Kent!" protested Minerva, looking right at her cousin. Was she going to tell some of her exaggerated stories again?

"But *chérie,* when I went back, it was almost as bad as in the war," Gabrielle smilingly protested, with a flutter of her white hands. She did it so beautifully, Minerva who had been copying the gesture felt like a very stupid amateur actress in the presence of a stage queen. "Poverty, hunger, bands of starving soldiers roaming the countryside—ready to attack one! Oh, I fair shivered! And then I married—it was well for a time. My dearest Gaspar protected me!" Complacently, she bit into a muffin, and sighed. "Food like this! Ah, sheer heaven! I remembered it in our worst times!"

Betsy Redmond poured more tea, added cream and sugar, and handed it across to Minerva. Minerva drank, she could not eat. She felt sick. Her revenge, shattered! Her plans, shot!

And her mother had done this to her. Reproachfully, Minerva stared at her mother, but Betsy refused to meet her daughter's gaze.

"Well, it was good of you to come, dear Gabrielle," said Mrs. Redmond. "You just dropped everything and came. I shall not forget it!"

Nor shall I, thought Minerva, resentfully. Betrayal! And at the hand of her mother!

"But I was ver' 'appy to come to you!" exclaimed Gabrielle with that bell-like, clear laugh that Minerva remembered so vividly. "I live in a little poor flat, with only memories about me! How delicious to come to dear

127

London, to stay with *mes chers* relatives and my dearest friends again! Do we go to Kent soon?"

"Not soon." Betsy Redmond smiled. "But that will be a story for later today. I have called off all appointments so we may visit *en famille!*"

Oh, dear, her mother was going all out, starting to speak French again, thought Minna mournfully. There was something about Gabrielle that made one want to imitate her, that made one catch her accent, listen with fascination to her drawl, observe her gestures, and wish to be as French as she!

She was fascinating as ever, though older. She must be only twenty-three, three years older than Minna, but she looked a matron, with wise green eyes and a knowing look to her. She had always been older than her years, and now it showed. Wrinkles around her eyes, just slight ones, perhaps from the night journey. Makeup skillfully around her mouth, but some lines there also.

"Gabrielle had a bad time of it with her husband," spoke François Claudel. "She will not admit it, but he was a brute!"

Minna gasped. Percy spoke up manfully.

"Oh, I say, you should have sent for me! I should have set him right!"

Gabrielle smiled brilliantly at Percy. "You are so kind," she purred, in that oh-so-familiar way. She had had men dropping at her feet like flies, as Minna remembered bitterly. All she had to do was purr! "But when one is marree—one must do as one's husband wishes! Gaspar lived accordingly as a Frenchman does—"

128

"That is rank slander," said François Claudel ruefully. "I would never lock you in a tower!"

They all stared at Gabrielle, even the maid serving them, in spite of her training unable to refrain.

"Locked in a tower!" gasped Minna, enthralled again, as always with Gabrielle. "He didn't!"

"Yes, several times." Gabrielle shrugged, her shoulders moving in a slight shudder. "The worst was the rats! And he fed me on bread and water."

Was she story-telling again? It was hard to know. Gabrielle could get away with the most outrageous lies. But again things had a way of happening to her! Minerva had always had difficulty figuring out whether Gabrielle was telling the truth. Just when she thought she had caught her in a lie, Gabrielle would pull the truth out of her bonnet, with dazzling smile, and proof.

"But why would he do that?" puzzled Betsy Redmond. "Was he ill, mentally deranged?"

"Oh, yes, at the last," agreed Gabrielle. "But he was always jealous of me. He thought I met men secretly, and he raged at me to tell him their names. He did not believe that I met nobody. I was faithful to him all our marriage," she said simply.

"And he did not believe you?"

"Not after his son turned him against me," she said. "He has a son, older than I, who lied about me. After Gaspar died, and the will was read, I realized why. Gaspar left me only the smallest of incomes. All else was left to his son, my stepson, who promptly turned me out of the house, and said 'go'!"

And she pointed dramatically to the nearest window, her black lace sleeve falling back from her white, beautifully formed arm.

"With no carriage, no trunks, no footmen," confirmed François Claudel, his strong teeth biting into toast.

"What did you do? The brute!" gasped Percy.

Gabrielle smiled. "I went to the neighbors, the most gossiping woman in the village," she said complacently.

Betsy Redmond laughed, Minna still gasped at her. "Oh, Gabrielle, you clever girl!" she said admiringly.

"Of course, it was all I could do. I had planned it, I had guessed, for his wife was so spiteful to me. As Gaspar lay dying, they moved into the château, and she began to rearrange the furniture. So I knew." And she nodded, her green eyes sad and wise.

"Because she rearranged the furniture?" asked Percy, his mouth hanging open, his body half across the table in his anxiety not to miss a word of the fascinating woman.

"Oh, yes. When a woman feels secure, she begins to take possession. Then she sets about making things the way she wishes them to be. Gaspar in the bedroom upstairs, where his father and grandfather and great-grandfather had died, and that bitch in the drawing room pushing my chaise longue farther from the fire, and her embroidery chair nearer to the fire screen! I knew then."

"And then as soon as he had died, and was buried, out she went," said François Claudel, his brown eyes more mournful. "I must say, this is excellent bacon! Even better than France!"

"Thank you, Monsieur Claudel," said Betsy Redmond demurely. "Allow me to ring for more. You must be starved, all that long journey."

He did not protest, she rang, the maids came with
130

more bacon, muffins, hot tea, thick Devon cream, chunks of sugar.

"So," continued Gabrielle, after a long satisfying sip of fresh hot tea. "I remained with the gossip until my stepson could endure the talk no longer. He allowed me to return with my friend, my lawyer, Monsieur Claudel," and she sent a dazzling smile to the man across the table from her. He half rose, bowed, and seated himself again.

"You returned to the château to live?" asked Minerva. She could not imagine returning so to the scene of such humiliation.

"Only to pack my dresses, my few jewels, some precious possessions of my parents, that is all. Then François drove me to Paris. He helped me to secure a flat—a tiny one—" she emphasized, with a wry smile. "So there I live now. I have a small allowance from my husband, I live on that. Of course—I may marry again."

She dropped that neatly into the silence. Minerva swallowed.

"There are some fine men in London," said Mrs. Redmond thoughtfully, idly drawing a pattern on the lace tablecloth with her finger. "We must introduce you to some friends of ours, Gabrielle. You will remain for a time?"

Gabrielle looked slightly surprised, then smiled warmly at her aunt. "Dear *Tante*, gladly! You are too generous! I am sick of my solitary living, fed up with my small company of acquaintances, weary of making do on my little income. If you will permit me to stay—" A shrug completed the answer.

"As you may surmise, there is a reason behind all this," Mrs. Redmond went on, sounding so much like a hard-headed Frenchwoman that Monsieur Claudel gazed at her in surprise. "My daughter Minerva has gotten herself into a little scrape. Nothing serious, but very awkward, and could cause some scandal. I am anxious to end the matter," she said sternly, glancing at Minerva.

"Minna is in trouble, *Minna?*" And Gabrielle turned to gaze intently at Minerva. "I cannot believe it! She is a good girl!"

It sounded like the most gross of insults to the sensitive Minna. "Well, I don't think you should be so surprised!" she flared. "I am twenty years of age, I am not a schoolgirl—"

"But, darling, you were always so *quiet!*" said Gabrielle, gently. Her black chiffon and lace gown floated as she leaned back in the chair, and studied Minna through half-closed green eyes. "No, you have not changed much. Your hair is better, I like it loose like that. We must do *something* about Minna."

She made it sound a desperate case. The worst of it was Minna could not fight her. She had never been able to fight Gabrielle. The girl was so clever, so sharp of tongue, so quick of mind.

"But what could have happened to *Minna?*" asked Gabrielle, with a slight frown. "You must tell me everything?"

"Later," said Mrs. Redmond. "You are weary from the journey. I will take you to your room, and see you settled. Tonight, we can talk. And I think we must enlist your aid, Monsieur Claudel! You can help us, I feel sure." And she gave him a smile that would have melted stone.

"I am at your service, *madame!*" he said promptly.

"I confess myself curious. I did not think the English became reckless and got into trouble! Just think of the cool Wellington! Your soldiers at Waterloo! *Ma foi,* we did not have a chance!" he said graciously.

Speaking of Waterloo reminded Minerva of Oliver, her lost, dear Oliver. What chance did she have now? And he was to have come at three, her battle would have been won—her revenge complete—the ending so sweet— All gone, gone, gone.

"Come, Minna, do not look so sad!" proclaimed Gabrielle, smiling at her cousin. "Come, you must tell me everything tonight! Then we will straighten out your little troubles, eh?"

Minna could not answer. She felt as she had so long ago. Gabrielle came, overwhelmed, conquered. She chatted, and everyone listened. She laughed, everyone smiled. She talked, one dared not interrupt.

She felt flat. In Gabrielle's presence, she had never shone. She had retreated, she had hidden under a blank face, she had been incapable of fighting back.

Gabrielle could sound so sweet and thoughtful, only a look in her cool green eyes revealed the truth. She cared about nobody but herself, she lived for nobody but herself. If she helped you, it was for some purpose of her own. She always came out a winner.

She overwhelmed one with ease. If Minna tried to answer, her words were turned against her like the curved sword of the fairy tales. She was made to feel a child, a silly infant. Silence was safer, and retreat into a corner. Minerva had always hated to look a fool, and Gabrielle did it to her so easily.

Minna had hated to be laughed at. When Minna defied Gabrielle, the cousin had always managed to

133

turn it about, and ended the incident with everyone laughing heartily at Minna. Minna had soon learned; she hid away from her cousin. She did not answer, she became the more quiet. And Gabrielle would tease her mercilessly about the times she hid in the bushes.

It was childhood all over again, thought Minna, as the luncheon table echoed with laughter. They were not laughing now at Minna—but they would. When Betsy Redmond told the story, Gabrielle would laugh again at Minna, she could not help it. Imagine, Minna masquerading as her French cousin! Imagine, Minna wearing French-design clothes, and alluring a wealthy beau.

Wealthy! The word echoed in Minna's mind. Oliver was very wealthy! She had forgotten!

Oliver Seymour had become to her the man she loved, the man she wanted to embrace her. The man she would marry, if possible!

But Oliver Seymour was very wealthy. Wait till Gabrielle caught sight of his gilded carriage and the two matched blacks! Wait till she saw Oliver in his golden silk coat and the sapphire rings he wore! And his jade collection! And his townhouse with the huge drawing rooms! And the Persian rugs! And the talk of his country estates!

And Gabrielle had her jade green eyes fixed on marrying a wealthy beau, perhaps someone younger and nicer than her elderly, mean Gaspar. Who could help wanting Oliver Seymour? Not Gabrielle! She would snatch him with both beautiful hands!

As the gay, sophisticated chatter went on, Gabrielle

did not seem at all weary. Minna had sunk into silence; she felt tired and dispirited, as though the battle was already over, and she had lost once more to her beautiful cousin.

Chapter 10

GABRIELLE CAME down to tea about four o'clock.
Oh, low blow—most bitter of sights—she was attired
in one of Minerva's new gowns, the silvery gray and
green stripe. It was too tight in the bust and hips, Minerva was pleased to see that. But Gabrielle wore it
well.

"I must call for Miss Clothilde to come and alter the
gowns for you, Gabrielle," said Betsy Redmond
thoughtfully. "Just a bit tight—a little more room in
the bust, I believe."

"It is so kind of you to give me these new dresses."
Gabrielle smiled dazzlingly. "I could scarce believe my
eyes when you and the maid brought them all in. And
new hats, and scarves—" She waved her hands appre-
ciatively.

Betsy Redmond had been firm with Minerva. "She
must have every gown you have worn these weeks,
Minna! You cannot appear in them again! And any
gown that is low cut, that is not for you!"

"But, Mama, I cannot go back to my pallid muslins,
my gray dresses—oh, Mama, I cannot! How can you
do this to me?"

"You did it to yourself," said her mother, ruthlessly.
Her gaze softened as she looked down at her daughter,
seated on the bed. "Come, darling, we will have more
gowns made. Miss Clothilde works very fast. I have

already sent her a note. She comes tomorrow to alter Gabrielle's gowns, and she will bring lengths for you to choose."

"But, Mama, these dresses—all my gowns—" Minna almost choked as she fingered the yellow silk for the last time.

"Too low cut! I was shocked at the time, but I held my tongue," said her mother firmly. "Now, you must return to your modest look, Minna! Brighter colors, yes, do not show your bosom! And you must not flirt so!"

"Gabrielle always did!" she snapped bitterly.

"Gabrielle is—Gabrielle. You are Minerva Redmond! And you are an English lady!"

"Yes, Mama."

When her mother spoke like that, with a bite in her tone, Minna retreated. The dresses were gathered up, the flirty hats, the scarves, all carried off to her cousin.

And she wore them so well!

"Yes, I was weary of black and gray, but I had little money to buy more! Of course, in Paris, black is always *très chic*," said Gabrielle, smoothing the green silk complacently. She managed to convey the thought that she enjoyed the dresses, but French chic was after all something else, something more to be desired than all the English gowns available.

François Claudel admired her frankly, with his sad monkey eyes. "You look beautiful whatever you wear, *chérie*."

"Merci, mille fois!" She sent an intimate, slow smile to him, and Minerva quivered. She sensed somehow that they were very close.

François had come all the way from Paris with her, he had been at hand to rescue her after her husband's

137

death. What was their relationship? Somehow, Minna, made more sensitive by her love for Oliver, quivered at the feeling in the air between the two of them. There was something that tied them together. Could they—be lovers?

She would watch and watch, she vowed. If Gabrielle set her sights on Oliver, and had been a mistress of François—well, Minna would have something to say about that! Only what?

Gabrielle noted her staring at François, and reached out to pat her hand. Minna turned, and saw the cool look of the jade green eyes, so like her own. Gabrielle was silently warning her, he is mine! Do not look! Possessive as ever, thought Minna, and smiled weakly back at her.

"Now, you must tell me zis so-troubling story, dearest Minerva!" commanded Gabrielle. "I am dying of curiosity! What kind of trouble have you gotten into, dear cousin?"

Minna sighed. The time of truth—and being laughed at—had come. "I have been masquerading as you, Gabrielle," she began bluntly.

The eyebrows raised, the eyes were surprised. "Impossible!" said Gabrielle, looking her up and down.

"Yes, I did," said Minna bravely. "I—I had bright clothes made, low cut, and I talked like you, with an accent—and pretended I had just come over from France."

"Um. But what happened to you, yourself? Did people not question?"

Betsy Redmond said, "We put it about that she was a-bed with a fever—chicken pox. Minna wished to pretend to be someone bright and gay and flirtatious, and attract a certain man of her acquaintance."

"Ah—a man!" Gabrielle nodded wisely. "Now it begins to make sense. Tell me about it!"

Minna, embarrassed over and over, told the whole story, though not what she had come to feel for Oliver. Gabrielle laughed of course, in her clear bell-tones, and mocked her, and wondered several times that people had been taken in. How could anyone really believe that Minna was *Gabrielle?*

"They did not know you," said Betsy Redmond. "Most of them had never met you."

Loyal Percy spoke up. "She was quite good with the French accent, you know, Gabrielle. And she does have a look of you! And when she is all dressed up, she is quite striking."

Gabrielle did not like that. Minna, sensitive to her every expression, noted the tightening of the mouth, the coldness of the jade eyes. There was only one Gabrielle Dubois, and she was an original of which there could be no true copy!

"Well, I am here now. I presume, dearest *Tante,* you wish me to take over the part, while Minna emerges from her illness, and we show the world there is a true French cousin?"

"Exactly, Gabrielle," said Betsy Redmond. "I feared that Minna could not get out of this trick without scandal. If you will be so kind, you will take over the part— which is you anyway, of course!—and Minna will be herself again. And of course you must stay in London as long as you will, and enjoy yourself!"

"You are most kind. Well, well, the part will be a
139

challenge—to be Minna—and yet myself! How wide is your acquaintance?"

Minna had the humiliation of talking then of her friends, naming them, explaining who everyone was. And of course she must talk of Oliver Seymour without betraying herself. Gabrielle caught all that she said of him, memorizing it, Minna felt sure.

"A large townhouse, estates in Kent—why, he must have veree much money!" And the big jade eyes went from Minna to her mother.

"He is rather wealthy," said Mrs. Redmond cautiously. "He inherited the estates in a rather dilapidated manner, and has built them up, at the cost of much of the money he was left. But he works hard, and has control of the estates in an admirable way. He is fond of the country—"

"Um." Gabrielle had a little smile at the corner of her mouth. François was watching her alertly, his eyes the more sad. He understood her, thought Minna. He must know her well! "Well, I shall play this part, dear cousin! Do not worry, I will do it well! You will coach me for a time, but I will learn quickly! Now, when will we meet this—Oliver Seymour?"

"He invites us over for cards in three days," said Betsy Redmond placidly. "Before then, you will meet some ladies for tea, we will drive out, Miss Clothilde will come and alter your gowns. By the time you meet Mr. Seymour, you will be quite prepared. It is most kind of you, Gabrielle, to help us out this way!"

The pretty fingers flirted with the air. Her ways were so exquisite and lovely, thought Minna, watching her. Every gesture a perfection. Every smile attractive. Every word studied. Only the wise old eyes mocked.
140

And she but twenty-three! She had lived a lifetime in her years. Minna felt a very child next to Gabrielle.

Miss Clothilde came the next morning, with three of her girls. If they were amazed to find Madame Dubois needed her dresses altered in the bust and hips, to be let out so soon, they concealed their surprise. They were well paid to do so.

Minna had to watch as all her elegant new gowns were altered to fit Gabrielle, and the Frenchwoman sauntered around in them, looking so much more elegant to envious eyes. How she moved, how she spoke, how she smiled, how her fingers flirted, how her eyes slanted—

Minna had recovered from her illness, and must have some new gowns also. Miss Clothilde came to measure her, showing no surprise at the healthy color and the size of her client. She read off the measurements in a calm tone, and one of her little girls wrote them down.

She had brought lengths of fabric. Minna fingered them with a tight mouth. A subdued pink silk. A pallid yellow. A pale blue, very demure.

"Could I not have more bright colors, Mama?" she begged in a low tone. "Must an unmarried female always wear such pale colors? Denise Lavery sometimes wears bright colors!"

Miss Clothilde proved an unexpected ally. "I believe the styles are changing, Mrs. Redmond," she offered. "Young ladies are turning to brighter colors, and more rich fabrics, even before marriage. I even made a velvet dress the other week for one unmarried female—of course, she is almost thirty."

Mrs. Redmond hesitated, then agreed. "Very well, then, some silks rather than muslins, Minna has many muslins. And a little brighter colors—perhaps some green? And brighter blue? I don't believe red, no, no—that is too daring."

"And with her hair, not right," agreed Miss Clothilde. "She has a fine complexion, let us set it off. So young and pretty of skin—no wrinkles."

Minna was a bit set up by that, Gabrielle did have wrinkles! Perhaps from so much makeup. She eyed her face with more complacency in the long mirror at the dresser, and submitted to the fittings more happily.

Miss Clothilde must have felt sorry for her, for she went back to her shop at noon, then returned in the afternoon with more offerings of fabrics. And these were so lovely that Minna felt better.

A length of jade green silk, to be made up demurely with rounded neck and a bit of Brussels lace at the throat to hide the bosom.

A length of pretty rose silk that did not clash with Minna's hair, to be made up as an evening gown, a bit lower in cut than her old dresses, though not so low as Gabrielle's.

A yellow silk that almost reconciled her to the loss of her other one, as a walking dress, with brown Spanish braid in a clever design at wrists and hem.

The little girls had remained and soon had the dresses altered for Gabrielle. She put on the yellow silk for tea that afternoon, as ladies were coming.

None of Minna's new gowns were ready, of course, and she must wear an old white muslin, with blue ribbons. But Minna rebelled at having her hair tied up tightly, and a muslin cap on her head.

"No more caps, not until I am an old lady!" she objected furiously, with some return of spirit. Jessie
142

seemed to agree, for she brushed out Minna's red-gold hair in a subdued version of the Madame Dubois style, in curls and ringlets, which were quite attractive, though not so wild as before.

She went down to tea, and was congratulated by the ladies for her recovery from her long illness. She told them it was chicken pox, she seemed able to lie very well by now. She had had to remain closeted until the last pox had disappeared, she told them. But she felt very well, I thank you, and able to take her place in society.

Gabrielle appeared, and was greeted so warmly that she was surprised. She managed her part graciously, but was bored by "old ladies," as she murmured later. She talked with them for a little while, but turned quickly to Percy and to François to carry on her flirtatious conversations, and tell veiled stories.

By some coincidence—Minna suspected her mother's contriving—their guests today were the same ladies who had been to tea on the day Minna had first appeared as Gabrielle. Mrs. Smythe-Jones turned to Minna.

"What a charming, intelligent cousin you have, Minerva!" she said kindly. "You must enjoy her company immensely."

"Actually, I have been ill, and seen little of her," said Minna distinctly. "And she is older than I, of course."

Mrs. Smythe-Jones looked rather shocked at the catty remark. "But surely only a few years."

"Yes—three years," Minna admitted. "But she is a widow, of course, and older in experience!" She felt furious, and ready to strike out. Her mother intervened.

143

"Minerva is still fretful from her illness. Do you wish to go up and lie down for a time in your room, darling?" Her look warned she would have no more of that.

"No, thank you, Mother, I feel quite well," she said, more meekly, and relaxed. She still felt betrayed. If Minna had had her way, she would be engaged to Oliver right this moment! Instead, she was expected to hand over her cousin to Oliver—indeed, deliver Oliver into those beautiful claws! She raged inside. Should she endure it, or could she fight and win, this time?

The younger Miss Jensen, a nice spinster of some forty years, left Mrs. Redmond's side, and approached Gabrielle as she lounged. "My dear Madame Dubois," she said timidly. "I wonder if you have considered helping me with the Literary Society tea this week? We will be speaking on the subject of Alexander Pope, comparing him to Samuel Johnson."

Gabrielle stared at her blankly, and lifted one shoulder. "Merciful heavens! I know nothing of such matters, and care less!"

It was a bad blunder. Minna cared deeply about those authors, and had carried on several enthusiastic conversations with Miss Jensen and Mrs. Peeples on the subject. There was a blank silence as all stared at Gabrielle in amazement. Minna had been half promised a membership in the Literary Society if only she remained in London! And now Gabrielle was showing her indifference!

Minna looked at her mother. She wanted to say, Get her out of this if you choose! But her mother only looked back, blandly. And Minna got the message.

If Minna was sufficiently mature to handle this, then she might have passed some sort of test.

"My cousin was much angered the other day by some insults to French writers, and this is her revenge," said Minna hastily improvising. "Of course, she is fond of the British writers, but the words that were said about Racine and Voltaire simply infuriated Gabrielle! Her loyalty to France and French writers has simply overcome her! Of course, we would *both* be delighted to come to the Literary Society tea!"

Her eyes dared Gabrielle to contradict her.

Miss Jensen beamed. "Oh, if only we might have Madame Dubois speak at her leisure—perhaps at the tea—and we would compare Racine to Pope! How splendid that would be! Perhaps next week, *madame?*"

Gabrielle swallowed and sat upright, jolted thoroughly for once, Minna was maliciously glad to see. So far as Minna knew, her cousin rarely opened a book.

"Oh, I cannot next week, I am so sorry! I am not prepared. And one should be thoroughly prepared for such an event. In Paris, I always spend three months studying, before daring to present a paper at our society teas!"

It was masterful, and Minna silently saluted her cousin. François Claudel seemed to have trouble, choking over his tea. He knew his Gabrielle.

"You are right, you are right," Miss Jensen was saying. "Of course one must prepare long for such an event, to do it properly. Forgive me!"

"Not at all," said Gabrielle graciously. "I hope your event goes well."

"We shall both come, and enjoy it," said Minna firmly. She meant to make Gabrielle suffer a little! She knew it would bore Gabrielle to tears!

But Gabrielle had the last word, as usual. As soon
145

as the ladies had swept out to their carriages, Gabrielle turned to Minna.

In her clear bell-tones she said, "How thoroughly bored I was by the tabbies! Minna, do not ever again put me in such a position! I am not amused by your malice! If you want me to play my part well, and not betray your little scrape, you will be very very good to me, eh?"

In the clear jade eyes, there was a threat and a promise. Minna swallowed. "Yes, Gabrielle," she said meekly.

"Good. You understand me. I do not want to have to be mean about this," said Gabrielle, and rose slowly. "I believe I shall go up to my room and rest before dinner."

She swept out. Mrs. Redmond said quietly, "Yes, that was not kind, Minna."

"I had to get her out of what Miss Jensen said!" protested Minna angrily. "I cannot help it if Gabrielle never reads!"

"She does not need to read, she knows everything about the human nature," commented François, with a dry smile, and left the room, taking the stairs two at a time.

Minna went on up to her room, also. She did not mean to sleep, she meant to look over her hats, and see if she could do something to them, now that Gabrielle had her new ones. But some sounds in the corridor soon drew her attention.

A man's footsteps. Had Percy come up to commiserate with her?

Cautiously she opened her door a crack, and peered out. Her eyes widened as she saw François Claudel pause at the door of Gabrielle's room.

Then the door opened, and a bare white arm reached out, to clutch his arm and draw him inside. A soft laugh—then the door shut.

Minna was left gaping. Had François come to talk to Gabrielle about something? She closed her door slowly—and waited. Uneasily, as she trimmed a hat, she listened—and listened—and listened. No sounds.

No door opening or closing.

No voices. She did hear a faint creak of bed springs several times.

Then she suddenly realized, and the girl gazed into space with wide green eyes.

Could they—be making love? Was François really the lover of Gabrielle?

And—in the afternoon! It was incredible! They were making love—in the afternoon!

Oh, those French people! Minna was so shocked and surprised, she scarce knew what to do. Should she tell her mother? Or keep silent?

Then her thoughts flew to Oliver Seymour. She could not endure it if Oliver kept on being attracted to Madame Dubois! Not if Madame Dubois was now really Madame Dubois!

He could not—could not—love Madame Dubois! He could not love Gabrielle! He could not court Gabrielle!

It had been bad enough before, the cousin was a widow, sophisticated, flirtatious.

But the real Gabrielle was so much worse, so much more cold and selfish—and she had a lover!

Minna could not allow it! She loved Oliver. She could not allow him to fall in love with the real Gabrielle!

She must save him, as well as herself!

She did not know how she could do it. But do it she must.

She must not only attract Oliver Seymour to herself, she must save him from Gabrielle Dubois!

Chapter 11

THE EVENING OF Oliver Seymour's card party arrived. It was a Wednesday. Miss Clothilde and her little girls had worked feverishly, like good fairies, and their handiwork was delivered in the afternoon.

Not only had they altered all the gowns for Gabrielle Dubois. One of Minna's new gowns had also arrived, the jade green silk with the Brussels lace.

Betsy Redmond advised Gabrielle to wear her jade silk also. "Then people will see you together, realize the likeness, and gradually accept Minna as she is," she said.

"But of course," said Gabrielle. "Though I am sure people will know she could not possibly be like me!"

"There is an amazing resemblance," said her aunt mildly. "But of course, you are very different!"

Gabrielle looked at her aunt suspiciously, but Mrs. Redmond's amiable face spoke of no malice or hidden meaning. "Naturally," said Gabrielle. "I am really French! And most mature in my thoughts and manners!"

She was never done with her little digs at Minna, especially since Minna had shown herself willing to be a rival. But this time, thought Minna, I shall not retreat! Oliver shall be saved from her!

Minna had found it difficult if not impossible to fight for herself against Gabrielle's subtle malice, but for

Oliver, she would fight! She loved him, and she would not see him delivered into Gabrielle's hands! She would hurt him very badly. And Minna would not endure that!

No, when it was necessary to fight, Minna had the courage to do so. It was a cause dear to her heart. Oliver, I shall not let you down, she vowed again and again.

She dressed in the jade green silk, and though it was a more modest gown than she had worn as Gabrielle, she was not unhappy at her look in the mirror. The color set off her clear, pale complexion, and her flaming red-gold hair. Jessie did her hair very carefully, not in the wild curls and tendrils as before, but a more modest version, in gentle waves down her back.

Jessie also did Gabrielle's hair, in a version of Minna's as Madame Dubois. When they stood side by side, they looked like cousins, but Minna looked like an innocent girl, and Madame Dubois like her worldly cousin from France.

"Amazing," murmured François, looking from one to the other. "I would not have credited it. What a difference a gown and hair style make! Minna does look like you, dear Gabrielle!"

"Of course, we are first cousins," admitted Gabrielle. She stared critically over Minna, but could find nothing to fault, though she did reach out and twitch the skirt into shape. "Yes, not too much makeup, you are not yet married, you know. What about a ribbon in her hair?"

A ribbon would make her look a schoolgirl again. Minna sent a desperate look to her mother. "I think the Spanish mantilla is fine," said Betsy. "Do let us start, or we shall be late!" And she started for the door.

Minna followed her with relief. She had a strong

feeling that after several days in Gabrielle's company, her mother was already looking forward to the departure of her guest. Gabrielle and her selfish concern only for herself could be very wearing.

They drove to the townhouse of Oliver Seymour. As the carriage rolled up into the semicircle of graveled drive, Minna heard Gabrielle catch her breath.

"This is his townhouse?" she asked sharply. "It seems very grand!"

"Yes, this has been in possession of the Seymours for a couple hundred years," answered Percy. "And they have a big place in Kent. Lots of work, but it looks well kept up."

When they walked into the grand hallway, onto the Persian rugs, Gabrielle looked around shrewdly. As though, thought Minna, she were mentally adding up what everything cost. She resented it, and feared it, this money madness of Gabrielle's.

Their host came to meet them, then stopped short, gazing from Gabrielle to Minna and back again. "My word! I had not realized how much alike you are!" he breathed. His gray eyes were very sharp, surveying them. Minna could not help shrinking a little. The last time she had seen him as Minna, he had insulted her. And she had been wearing something schoolgirlish and musliny.

He turned then to her mother, and greeted her cordially. "How splendid to see you again. And how happy you must be that your daughter is restored to health once more!"

"A great relief," said Mrs. Redmond demurely. "It did linger so long, that fever!"

He then turned to Gabrielle, and looked keenly into

her face. She was smiling, looking at him over her fan, in the familiar manner that Minna had tried to copy. But nobody could quite imitate that flirtatious look, the sly slant of the green eyes over the black Spanish fan. Minna could not keep laughter from her eyes. Gabrielle did not laugh, she was serious, and the look went over his face, down over his body to his boots, and up again. It was a purely feminine look, knowing and mature.

Oliver blinked, then bowed slightly. He did not reach out for her hand, as he always had to Minna. "Good evening, Madame Dubois," he said quietly.

"Good evening, Mr. Seymour."

Minna went stiff. She had come to call him Oliver, she had forgotten to warn Gabrielle about that. She exchanged a quick look with her mother; Betsy Redmond shook her head ever so slightly. There was nothing they could do at the moment. Of course, he might think it was a teasing formality.

"You look magnificent—as always," he said. His look went to her bosom, half exposed by the low-cut jade green silk, the lace. Would he note that her bosom was more full? Would he see the wrinkles about her eyes, the thicker black makeup around her eyes?

"I zank you, *monsieur!*"

There. That accent. Minna had caught that! She had imitated it perfectly, she thought proudly.

Oliver turned to Minna, and held out both hands. Shyly, a little surprised, she put her hands in his. "And dear little Minerva," he said tenderly. "You are well at last! How glad I am to see you tonight! You look spendid!"

"Thank you, Oliver," she said, and blushed. She had
152

not meant to use his name like that. "I mean—Mr. Seymour."

"No, no, we are friends, are we not? You have my flowers?"

"Yes, you were most kind to send them so often."

The keen eyes went over her slowly. "And you have changed," he said naturally. "How pretty you look. You have changed your hair style, I believe." And he smiled.

Was there mischief in his gray eyes? Yes, there was. Did he guess? He could not! Yet—

"Yes. While I was ill so long, and it was so very boring! I decided to brighten up. My cousin kindly advised me about more flattering styles of hair—and dress," she said bravely, not daring to look at Gabrielle.

"Very charming, and so kind of your cousin," he said. "Yes, yes, I do approve. And was your illness so very miserable?"

"Oh, it had its moments," she said, looking up demurely into his eyes. She could not help it! She had become accustomed to flirting with Oliver, and it was so very tempting to continue!

He blinked again, looked more keenly at her, and smiled down into her eyes. "I am sure," he murmured. "I expect you read a great deal. You are so fond of reading."

"Yes, I read—Percy brought me many books from the lending library. He is so good to me! And I refinished some hats—"

Gabrielle interrupted. "All this is most interesting, I am sure. But there are persons behind us, dear Minna!"

Her cold, clear tones, shocking as a dash of water,

parted them. Minna gulped, and shrank back from Oliver.

Oliver gave Gabrielle a sharp look. "Thank you for reminding me of my duties," he said, and only Minna seemed to realize there was sarcasm in his polite tones. Oliver was very aware of society, and very kind, she thought. He did not need such words!

He shook hands with Percy, was introduced to François Claudel, and gave him a long thoughtful look. "So this is your new guest from France," he said gently. "I was so sorry that his arrival—welcome though it was—prevented me from coming the other day, Gabrielle!"

She looked blank, then smiled brilliantly to cover the fact that she did not know what he was talking about. "But you are welcome any time!" she managed to say.

Minna did not bother to rescue her, she swept on to let the next guests speak to Oliver. Gabrielle caught her up, and put her arm around her.

"What was that?" she asked sharply. "You did not warn me?"

"Mr. Seymour was supposed to call upon me the day you arrived," said Minna. "Mother wrote him a note and asked him to postpone his visit. That is all."

"You should have told me," said Gabrielle, and pinched her arm sharply. "Do not be so forgetful!" And she moved on, smiling.

Minna felt such dislike of her cousin that she blithely deserted her and all their party. Mrs. Redmond had sent for Gabrielle, let her take care of her! Minna went off on her own, to greet her friends warmly, and receive their rapturous greetings.

154

Denise Lavery held both her hands. "You are well again, Minna! How happy I am to see you!"

"Thank you, Denise! You cannot believe how very happy I am to be quit of my bed! How dull I was! Thank you for your kind messages. Only my friends and their concern kept me from falling into the deepest doldrums!"

Mary came up to greet her warmly. "Your cousin Gabrielle was so sweet to me while you were ill, but we did miss you, dearest Minna. And how lovely you look tonight! I did not realize what a resemblance there is between you!"

Mrs. Charlotte Lavery followed her daughters over to greet Minerva. "How fine you look, Minna! I declare, your illness must have been good for you. A new gown? It becomes you well!"

"Thank you, Mrs. Lavery. And you were so good to send the custards and beef broth! They were all delicious. Yes, I am well again, and happy to be out. Thank you—thank you—" She was smiling, and greeting everyone, so happy she never thought to be her old, quiet head-for-the-corner self.

Ross Harmsworth came up to her, gazing in surprise. "I declare—is it little Minna Redmond? How fine you look! I heard you were ill. You are well again? May I have this dance?" And he held out his arm gallantly.

"Yes, I thank you. And how fine you look. Your uniform is so becoming—as you must know!" And she laughed up at him and his surprised look.

He blinked down at her. "I declare, you are a little flirt tonight, Minna! Come along. May I have the supper dance?"

"I will not say! It is a long time until supper, and you may meet a dozen prettier ladies!"

He threw back his head and laughed aloud. "You call me changeable, but so are you, little Minna! You look lovely tonight. I say, your illness must have changed you!"

"I did feel rather dowdy," she said demurely. "I decided I must change. And the fashions are changing, you know, the styles are much more bright!"

He looked blank. "Wouldn't know about that, miss! But I like that gown on you. Pretty color, matches your eyes!"

"Thank you, Captain!"

She found it so easy to talk to him, whereas he had always overwhelmed her with his heavy gallantries. And later she danced with Teddy Bailey, stammering and red-faced, and told him how she had missed him. He beamed and hummed and hawed, but asked her at once for the next dance she had free.

She turned from him, smiling, and a hand caught her arm. She looked up, she knew that touch. And Oliver Seymour was smiling down at her.

"May I have this one?" he asked softly, and put his arm about her before she could say yes or no. "I have asked for a waltz!"

And sure enough, the orchestra was playing, and she danced with him as in a dream. In the next room, her mother was playing cards, and looking over at Minna in a wondering way. And Gabrielle was dancing with François, looking annoyed at something.

"I did not know there would be dancing tonight," said Minna breathlessly.

"I had decided when I could not see you several days

ago. You were out of bed, they said, and well again, but I was not allowed to call. So I decided that your first event outside the house must be at my home. Are you enjoying youself, Minna?"

He had never spoken so to "Minna," and she was at once wary and confused. Did he know who she was, did he guess about the masquerade? He could not! It was impossible! Yet it was delicious to be uncertain, the danger was delightful.

"It was—most kind of you—to think of this," she said, breathlessly. "Th-thank you for your thoughtfulness. I am so happy to be—well again—"

"You stutter a little, as your cousin Gabrielle does at times," he said. "I had not noticed that before."

"Oh, we are much alike—that is, outwardly," she said hastily.

"She is a very changeable person," said Oliver. "We became quite well acquainted the past three weeks. Yet tonight she does not seem to remember some matters we had talked about."

Oh, heavens! Minna went still with fright, and lost her step. He caught her more strongly by the waist, held her against him for a long moment, so she felt him all down her slim body.

"Did you slip?" he asked softly.

"Y-yes. I'm so sorry."

He held her, then, and she finally got her step again, and they went sailing on in the waltz.

"I was able to add to my jade collection," he said, as the dance ended and the orchestra members paused to wipe their moist brows. He tucked her hand in his arm. "Come and see what I purchased at the auction."

She went with him gladly. They paced through the

157

drawing rooms, from one to the other. Most were filled with little tables at which the older people and some children were playing loo and whist. She shook her head, smiling, when she was invited to stop and play with them.

"Not just now, perhaps later," she said.

Oliver commented, idly, "You seem to have lost some of your shyness, Minna. I am glad to see it. Perhaps being out of the world for a time was good for you! You appreciate your friends more."

"Ah—I believe I do," she said sweetly, clutching her fan tightly with her free hand. Was she betraying herself? Should she act more as she had in the past? No, she did not want to be like that shy old Minna! "I did miss people. Being alone all the time is not very comfortable! With the chicken pox, one is not supposed to see people, you know."

"Very contagious, I understand. I hope you were not in pain, dear Minna?"

They had come to the room with the jade collection. He stepped over to a case, and taking a key from his pocket he opened the glass door.

"Oh, no, no pain, just the fever," she said. "Oh, how beautiful!"

He had taken from the case a statue about ten inches tall, in green jade, of a Chinese goddess with a sweet face.

"This is a Kuan Yin statue," he told her. "She is the Goddess of Mercy. The Chinese are very fond of her, and I think I shall be also."

He put the statue in her hand, and she caressed it gently. The jade was cool and smooth to the touch, except where it was carved for the little hands and feet.

158

The face was exquisite, the expression serene and sweet. Minna studied the face intently.

"She looks—merciful," said Minna. "I think she looks something like the statues in the Roman Catholic churches, of the Virgin Mary. Perhaps that is a universal wish, for a goddess that is merciful and loving."

"Yes, I believe it may be," he said. "It certainly appears in a number of religious beliefs. A mother figure. Someone who loves one no matter how naughty one is. Surely your mother and mine are like that, don't you think so?"

She started and blushed. Certainly she had tried her mother's patience these weeks! "I suppose so," she mumbled. "Does your mother have much to forgive you, Oliver?" she then said, flickering a glance up at him mischievously.

He laughed softly, and put the Kuan Yin back in the case. He took out another figure, an animal, and put that in her hand. "Not recently," he said enigmatically. "Do you like this?—a horse, like those the Mongols rode. Look at his head, the warlike carriage of it—"

She admired it very much. She also admired other things he showed her, a pink jade vase, a white mutton-fat jade carving of a whale, a huge jade piece of a house and garden like those of China.

"I have not yet found the French jade pieces I wish to add to my collection," he said seriously, as he carefully set back the last pieces.

Minna glanced at him quickly. Was he serious, or did he tease her? Was he speaking in double meanings? Did he know she had pretended to be Gabrielle? He had said that about the French jade to Gabrielle!

"Indeed," she said, inadequately. "I hope you find
159

what you wish," she added politely, and turned to leave as he offered her his arm.

Instead, he bent down, and his lips smoothed her cheek. "How glad I am that you are well again, Minna. I have missed you," he said kindly.

She caught her breath. He need not sound so like a—a brother!

"Thank you, Oliver," she said, rather forlornly. He half smiled, and turned her face up to his with his strong hand.

"And did you miss me?" he whispered, and set his mouth firmly on hers. He kissed her tentatively, as though tasting her mouth. Then he moved his lips more firmly over hers, and she felt the familiar thrill go down her spine, as his free hand moved over her back down to her hips.

She did not rebuke him, and he noted that. He was grinning when he stood erect, and his gray eyes sparkled.

"Yes, you have changed, Minna," he said. "You would not have allowed me to kiss you—before your illness! I highly recommend fevers to young shy girls!"

She gasped at his boldness, and the double meaning—if that was what it was.

"Indeed—you caught me by surprise," she said feebly.

"I must do it again!" he said, and took her arm to escort her back to the drawing rooms. She went with him in a daze. She did not know how to act. Gabrielle Dubois could allow kisses, and bold words. She was a widow, and no innocent girl. But Minerva Redmond—that was another matter!

160

Oliver brought her to one room where Denise Lavery and Percy played cards with another lady.

"We need a fourth, Minna," said Denise, with a smile. "Do come and join us." She indicated the empty chair at their table.

"Thank you, I will," and Minna sat down there. Oliver bowed and left them. Minna could not help looking after him as he moved gracefully, bowing to one, speaking to another.

They shuffled the cards, dealt them, but all seemed more interested in conversation than in cards. Percy was quite poor at cards tonight, he seemed intent on Denise's lovely face and her words.

"Where is your cousin, Madame Dubois, tonight?" asked Denise presently. "You do not hang on her shoulder tonight, Percy!"

He started and flushed. "There is no need." He shrugged giving Minna a wary look. "She knows everybody here."

"Oh?"

"And besides," said Minna quickly, "her beau came from France, Monsieur Claudel. He escorts her all about. They are old friends."

"Oh, I see," said Denise thoughtfully.

"I feel quite free—to—ah—dance with whom I wish, and play cards, and all that," said Percy hopefully. "Not a worry in the world!"

"Indeed?" and Denise gave him a mischievous sideways look of her pretty violet eyes. "No worries at all, Percy? What a heavenly state of mind!"

Minna chuckled, and Percy turned beet red. "Well—that is—I would not if—I mean—"

Minna rescued him, loving her brother's look of help-

161

lessness. He was a dear good man. "Only one or two, which I am sure can be resolved with some good will," she said smoothly. *"He* is not a flirt, *he* knows his mind, *he* is not easily swayed by fashions of the moment. I am sure Percy knows his own mind always, and is faithful to his—family and those he loves."

"What an excellent tribute from a sister to a brother," said the older lady with them approvingly. "Six—seven—eight—I do believe I have won the hand!"

She had; the other three had paid no attention to their cards. She presently departed, to find people more intent on gaming than on love affairs.

Just then, Oliver Seymour came through with Gabrielle swaying on his arm. She looked triumphant, a sly smile on her lips as she caught Minna's look. Oliver gave Minna and Percy a bright smile.

"Well, I never—" muttered Percy indignantly as they went on through. "Is he so fickle then? He just took you away, Minna, and now he—ouch!"

She had kicked him hard under the table. He went red again, under his red thatch of hair, and rubbed his leg.

"You don't have to kick me, Minna. Denise knows what's what," he said furiously. "Excuse me." And he got up and went away.

Minna sighed. "I am wrong again," she said. "Percy is not underhanded. He would rather come right out and say something, than to take sly hints and nudges and kicks under the table!"

"Yes, he is ever honest and honorable, and hates lying and deceit, it is one of his many admirable traits," said Denise, laying the cards on the table. "Minna—would you tell me frankly—"

162

"Oh, yes?" encouraged Minna, as the other girl paused.

There was a becoming pink in the pretty cheeks. "I think—sometimes—that Percy likes me—more than a little. Yet, he did escort your cousin about so devotedly for two weeks. Is he—does he—feel his duty so?"

"Yes, he does," said Minna decidedly. "I know he regretted that he had to spend so much time with her, but he felt it his solemn duty! She was our guest, and I was—unable to be with them." She could not say to the serious violet eyes that she had been sick. "But I know he is devoted to you, Denise," she added softly.

"Oh, is he? I have felt—I know my own heart, but it is so difficult to know the heart of another," sighed Denise, frankly. "You are close to Percy, you know him, even more than most sisters know most brothers—"

"Yes, and he loves you dearly," said Minna bluntly. "I know that because Percy is so frank, he has told me so! And Mother also! We know his dearest wish is to win your hand. He wished first to get the estates in order, and he has worked so hard. And he wanted you to have your seasons in London, and have fun before you were married and tied down. Yet he wishes to speak his heart to you, I know it."

"Oh, Minna, you are simply—splendid!" said Denise, pressing her hand to Minna's on the table. "I wish every girl had a man with a sister such as you! It would be so much easier! And he is a fine man, is he not? He has no vices, you would tell me!"

"Well, his bluntness can be uncomfortable," said Minna. "He does not hesitate to tell me when I displease him! But he does not sulk. He is frank and honest. He

163

would never lie to me or to Mother. He works hard, as hard as any of his men. And he would lie down and die for any of us, if it would do any good, he has said it. But I think he would rather stand up and fight for us! That is more his style!"

"Oh, I know it! Percy is wonderful!" breathed Denise, starry-eyed. "I do wish he would speak to me—and to Papa!"

"I do too," said Minna. "Shall I speak to him?"

Denise gave a little shriek, blushing wildly. "Oh, I pray you, do not! Oh, I am so embarrassed—here he comes!" And she put her hands to her hot cheeks.

"Don't worry—I won't if you don't want—" Minna reassured. "But do encourage him, Denise! Smile at him, for heaven's sake!"

Denise gave Percy a wavering smile as he brought the tray to the table and set it down. "Something cool to drink, how lovely," she quavered.

"I asked the waiter for some punch without liquor," he said cheerily. "The other stuff is too strong for words! Minna would fall down under the table, I'm sure!" And he handed the glasses to them.

Minna laughed, and thanked him.

"Oh, you are kind," said Denise fervently. "I am always afraid to try the punch myself. Papa usually does it for us. Umm, this is delicious, and so cool!"

"Well, anytime you want me to try the punch for you, just say so," said Percy gallantly. "Happy to oblige," and he looked at her with his heart in his green eyes.

François Claudel came up behind Minna. "Where is Madame Dubois?" he asked.

Minna almost choked on her punch.

164

"She is with Mr. Seymour," said Percy. "They went that way." He pointed.

François looked furious, but finally sat down with them, and glared down at the cards. "She is very enchanted with him," he said bitterly.

Minna felt the same way, but could not say it. Oliver and Gabrielle had been gone quite a time. Gabrielle must have seen how wealthy he was, the house, the sapphires on his hands, the elaborate party he gave, besides the decorations of the house. And his jade collection. Was he showing Gabrielle his jade? Or kissing her?

Denise kindly encouraged François to join in a game of cards with them.

"How much are the stakes?" he sighed, then, picking up his cards.

"Not for money, just for fun," said Percy bluntly.

"Oh—really?" said François. "Very well. The English have strange habits," he remarked, half to himself.

"Keeps one's friends," said Percy, to him. "I've known many a silly fight to start over wagering. Doesn't do, you know. Not worth it. Rather keep my friends."

"You are a good man," said François.

"I think so too," said Denise softly. Minna noted with satisfaction when Percy's fingers went slowly over to Denise's, and pressed hers for a moment.

François noted it also, and raised his eyebrows briefly to Minna. She nodded. He was very perceptive.

"I was more fortunate," said Percy, clearing his throat. "I do not know what I would have done without my father's presence, his advice and wise counsel. He told me about the estates from an early age, I always
165

went with him when I was home from school. When he—died—and I had to take over—I was more prepared than most men would have been."

"I wonder if he knew—or had some premonition—" said Denise soberly.

"I don't think so. He just believed in being prepared," said Percy. "I shall treat my children so," he added firmly.

Denise blushed, and raised her fan of cards to her face briefly. Minna half smiled to herself, and bid.

The play went on idly. All were more interested in their conversation, and Minna was watching more and more anxiously for Oliver to return with Gabrielle from the other rooms.

Then her mother and Mrs. Seymour returned, looking grave. They paused once more at the card table. François and Percy jumped up, but the ladies refused the seats.

"No, no, be seated again, please. Who is winning?" But Betsy Redmond did not seem concerned much with the play.

"François is," said Percy. "He has a keen mind, and I think he memorizes all the cards played!"

"And I am unlucky in love," sighed François.

A footman came through the rooms, bowing, announcing that supper was served. Several guests rose, to make their way to the buffet.

Percy turned to Denise. "May I have the pleasure of your company for the supper?" he asked.

She smiled, and put her hand on his arm as she rose. François glanced nervously toward the other rooms, where Oliver and Gabrielle had disappeared. He was

166

about to turn to Minna and her mother, when Gabrielle and Oliver were seen.

Minna saw them first, and her jaw went tight. Gabrielle was definitely mussed, her hair in a glorious tangle. And as they came closer, Minna saw a smear of lipstick on Oliver's jaw. They had been kissing.

Something exploded in her. Gabrielle should not have him! He was too fine, too good for someone like her! He deserved better! If he was not for Minna, at least she would save him for someone else in the future!

Mrs. Seymour and Mrs. Redmond turned also and saw them approach. They did not seem surprised, but Minna caught the look of uncertainty and disapproval in Mrs. Seymour's face. Oliver smiled gaily at his mother, his arm holding Gabrielle's hand tightly to his vest.

"Ah, here you are," he said in what could only be called a jolly manner. "Supper is announced, and I must admit I am starving! Gabrielle, will you do me the honor?"

And they went off together. Minna stared after them, then took one of François's arms in silence. Her mother took the other. Mrs. Seymour went with Percy and Denise. All were quiet, thinking.

The food was delicious, but it might as well have been bread and water to Minna. She nibbled at the veal pasties, ate a peach, drank some champagne recklessly, then went off to dance with Teddy Bailey. She laughed a lot—probably the champagne—because she felt miserable.

She kept seeing Oliver's head bent over Gabrielle's red locks. In spite of his very polite manners, he danced with that one guest half the evening, and people were whispering.

Gabrielle was triumphant! But it was not her triumph, Minna kept telling herself. It was Minna who had paved the way. It was Minna who had attracted him. It was Minna who, dressed as Gabrielle, had drawn him these weeks. And now Gabrielle Dubois was getting all the attentions from him! It was not fair!

She was dancing with an older man, when Oliver paused beside her. "Minna, may I have the next dance?" He smiled kindly, as though to a child. "I meant to celebrate your return to us!"

She smiled, and went into his arms at the beginning of the next dance. But he held her at arms' length, and looked at her in the old way, half mockingly, half nicely.

"Well, well, little Minna is growing up!" he said.

Between her nice pearly teeth, she bit out, "I am grown up! I am twenty!"

"So you are, so you are," he said, as though a child had told him she was three and three-quarters years old. "And you have no ill effects from your long sickness?"

She wished he would stop harping on that sickness! She was heartily sick of her sickness.

"I am fine," she snapped. He reached out and touched her forehead for a moment.

"You sound as though you might be taking a fever once more, you are quite cross," he murmured, solicitously. "Do you feel hot, Minna?"

She did, but not from sickness. It was from being near to his warm masculine body.

"The room is a trifle warm," she muttered.
168

"You must take care, perhaps you should go home early!" he suggested.

"I will not!" she cried. "I have not been out for ages— I mean—I am all right—and I won't go home early!"

She really did feel as though she had been sick, and deprived of society for three weeks. Such is the power of the imagination.

"Now, now, do not be upset," he soothed, with a charming smile. "You shall stay up as late as you wish! But do sleep late tomorrow, and get your rest, Minna, dear!"

She could have slapped him. He drew her closer, and swung her easily in the waltz. But he moved her almost impersonally, not the way he had done when she was Madame Dubois. Oh, she missed it! She wanted to be the Merry Widow again, bold and flirtatious, and inviting his caresses!

But Gabrielle had that role now, and adored it! She would not give it up!

He let her go with a bow, made sure she had another partner, then went back to Gabrielle Dubois, who received him with a radiant, triumphant smile. She had never had such an easy victory, thought Minna, viciously, dancing slowly with her elderly partner.

Then she saw Percy beckoning to her from the next room. He had Denise on his arm, and both looked radiant. She made her way through the crowd as her partner bowed and left her.

Many were dancing; they were alone in the little drawing room next to the ballroom. Denise looked at Percy.

Percy beamed down at his sister, he seemed unable to speak.

"Well, what is it? Do you wish to go home?" teased Minna, with a sparkle in her eyes.

"No!" he blurted out, turning red. "I wanted to—that is, I asked her!"

"You asked her what?" said Minna, tapping his arm with her fan. "Did you ask her to dance?"

Denise giggled. "He asked me, Minna!" she murmured.

"Dear me, what did he ask?"

Percy finally managed to say, "Asked her to marry me! Said she would!"

"But we cannot announce it, Papa has not been asked!" whispered Denise hastily.

"Wanted you to know, Minna, dear," said Percy simply. "You helped!"

Deeply touched, Minna leaned to Denise and they kissed. "I am so very happy, dearest Denise," she said. "I could not ask for a sweeter sister!"

"Nor I, and I have three!" smiled Denise. "Oh, and I know Papa will consent! He thinks Percy is wonderful, as I do!" And she sent an adoring look up to Percy.

"I'll come tomorrow morning and ask him. What time does he arise?" asked Percy seriously.

Denise smiled, a becoming pink in her cheeks. "I think if you come about ten o'clock, Percy, he will receive you," she said.

"Ten? I shall not sleep all night!" he said.

"If you do sleep deeply, I'll come and waken you," teased Minna, and they all laughed. "Oh, Mother will be so happy about this," she said. "She loves you, Denise."

Denise was immensely pleased with this message,

and said, "You are so kind to me! Oh, I shall be happy in your family, I know it!"

Percy presently asked Denise to dance with him, and they went off blissfully. Her radiant looks up at Percy, his adoring looks at her, the way he held her so—so protectively and gently—made Minna feel happy for them.

They did truly love, it was evident, and theirs would be a marriage of true minds. They were both warm-hearted, sweet of nature, and earnest about work and their duties in life. It would be a good marriage, and she was so happy for her brother.

Then her glance fell on another couple, and she felt rather blighted. Oliver and Gabrielle were dancing again. Did Gabrielle have no regard for her reputation, that she accepted him so often? But Minna knew it was sour grapes for her, she would willingly have traded places with her cousin.

Oliver saw her, and smiled. He said something to Gabrielle, who did not look pleased, however they both came to Minna standing alone in the doorway to the ballroom.

"You look lonely," said Oliver. And that is the worst thing one can say to one feeling a wallflower.

She stretched her mouth in an unconvincing smile. "Oh, no, I am just resting from dancing so much."

"You are weary," said Oliver at once, with a worry line on his forehead. "Minna, you should go home. I will speak to Percy at once."

"Oh, no, I pray you, do not do that," she said hastily. Not for the world would she interrupt that happy couple. "I am fine, I tell you!"

"Do not be cross," said Gabrielle, her eyes narrowing.

"Dearest Oliver, could you not send her home in one of your carriages? I feel sure she is doing too much!"

Minna could have killed her cousin cheerfully, stabbed her in her full bosom.

"You are very kind to her," he said, gazing down at Gabrielle. "How good it is to see cousins so close and so fond of each other! I believe you lived together for three years?"

"Yes, and we became like sisters." Gabrielle smiled.

Oh, liar, black dreadful mean liar, thought Minna vengefully.

"That is a good idea, to send Minna home," said Oliver. "I will get one of my footmen to take her. Let me see—" And he began to look about.

"No, I will not go!" said Minna, feeling like a cross child being sent to bed. "I am—having—fun—a wonderful time—and I—am—not—weary!"

"Dear me, Minna, your old temper is coming out!" tutted Gabrielle. "I well remember when she was younger, how she used to scream and then hide in the bushes. Remember, Minna, how you hid in the bushes, to keep from going to bed?"

Minna literally could not prevent it. A demon made her say it.

"Oh, it was not to keep from going to bed, Gabrielle!" she answered sweetly, and clearly. "I liked hiding in the bushes, to watch you manage your beaux! You always got them to kiss you in such interesting ways! It was very—fascinating! You were but sixteen, I recall, when Peter Carmichael got you in the maze, and—"

Gabrielle had her mouth open unbecomingly when Oliver intervened, incredulously. "Minna, be quiet! I am amazed at you! How can you say such things!"

Was it anger and fury in his gray eyes? Or was it an unholy amusement? She could not tell, and she dared not stare at him.

Gabrielle found her tongue. She was an unbecoming red. "I declare, what a liar you have become, Minna! I shall speak to *Tante* about this!"

"Do—I dared not tell her at the time, Gabrielle. But I do feel you should confess to Mother! She was responsible for you!"

Gabrielle gasped, and gave Minna such a look, Minna knew she would be in for a bad time when they were alone. But recklessness drove her on.

Oliver intervened hastily. "Come now, no more of this. Gabrielle, I meant to ask you—would you come driving with me tomorrow? I mean to drive into the countryside, I think you would enjoy it. I can arrange for a fine nuncheon at an inn, to make the journey less wearisome."

Minna was outraged. That invitation should have come to her! She had to stand and be quiet as Gabrielle smiled up alluringly at Oliver and replied, "I should adore it, Oliver! How kind you are to ask me! What time shall we depart?"

"May I come for you at eleven o'clock? And do bring a bonnet and shawl, it will probably be cool by the time we return in the evening!"

To take her out all day—alone—he made no mention of a chaperon! Minna's temper, none too steady by now, was about to topple over and crash!

"It sounds like a lovely journey, Oliver. How kind you are to think of it! I shall be ready!" And Gabrielle could not refrain from giving Minna a long, significant, triumphant look.

173

"Jessie will be glad to come with you, she loves the carriage rides," suggested Minna sweetly.

Gabrielle did not even need to say a word.

"No, no," said Oliver quickly. "She will not need Jessie! I am sure your aunt will approve! She has known me for years!"

A dreadful fear came over Minna. He meant to propose to Gabrielle Dubois! Oh, she must prevent it, she must! Oliver had marriage on his mind!

And he had only met Gabrielle this evening! He did not know it, but he had only just met Gabrielle! He had no idea of what she was really like!

She must prevent this horrible mistake! She had even reached out to clutch Oliver's arm when she realized she could not say anything. She was in a trap of her own making. She could not expose herself this way.

Oh, what a coil Minna was in!

While she had stood silent, the two others had been speaking, making further arrangements for the next morning. Oliver would come at eleven, he would have the comfortable carriage with the hood over the front seat. She did not need to wear riding habit, a dress would do. He would order the luncheon in advance, was there any food she particularly wished? Chicken, splendid. And white wine, yes, of course. And pâté—of course. And pastries, naturally.

Minna's heart swelled in indignation as Oliver named off all her favorite foods—chicken, oyster pâté, chocolate and almond puff pastries—and Gabrielle should have them!

Betsy Redmond appeared at Minna's side. Her sharp

174

look went around to them all. "Having a good time, darlings?" she asked cheerily.

Minna could have wept.

"Oh, yes," murmured Gabrielle, giving Oliver a melting look. "Monsieur Seymour entertains so delightfully! I am so enchanted. How happy I am! How glad I came to London, dull though it can be! It was so sweet of you to invite me, *chère Tante!*"

Minna could not smile. Her mother made all the conventional replies, and urged Minna with her.

Oliver put his arm about Gabrielle and they began to dance again.

Mrs. Redmond whispered, "Darling, it is for the best! If he likes her so much—"

"I will never forgive you for sending for Gabrielle! He liked me best! And he does not know what she is like!"

"Dearest, he is an older man, if he likes a more experienced woman, that is his privilege! You are but twenty—"

"Oh, Mother! She is not right for him," said Minna, shaking her head. "She will make him miserable! She has no loyalty—she betrayed her husband, she would again."

Mrs. Redmond looked surprised, then thoughtful. "But he is a stronger man, I feel sure. He would keep her in line—"

"Would you want Percy to marry a woman who has a lover?"

Betsy Redmond gasped at her daughter's frank words. "A lover?" she whispered, glancing about her warily.

"François."

175

"Oh, dear!" She gulped. "Are you sure?"

"I have seen him go into her room—afternoons and nights."

"You should not have looked," said her mother automatically. "And he stayed?"

"Hours."

"Mercy." Mrs. Redmond looked rather helpless.

"Well, Mother," said Minna. "You have to expect it. She has been married. And she is French. And she always did like lots of attention from different men."

They had to stop talking about this. Astrid Faversham had come within speaking distance. She was smiling, obviously a false smile, for her cold gray eyes surveyed them haughtily.

"I see your niece has captured Mr. Seymour," she said, in a snap of her teeth. "He dances with her all night!"

"Not quite," said Minna. "He danced with me also!"

"Duty dances," said Astrid, and it was almost a cry. *"She* has him in her palm!"

"I hope not," muttered Minna fiercely.

"Well, it is only my first season, and there are other men," said Astrid. "Only—it would have been such a cachet, to capture someone like him the first season!"

Minna drew herself up. "My dear Astrid," she said firmly. "It would be a great privilege and high honor— to marry someone like Oliver Seymour—in any season!"

"Well said," her mother commented, and patted her arm. Astrid looked rather shocked, then subdued.

"I guess you are right, Miss Redmond," she said, meekly for her. "It has been an education—Mother said so—to come to know Mr. Seymour—and you, of course,
176

Mrs. Redmond, and Minerva. And your cousin." And she went off, her head held high.

"For once," said Betsy Redmond. "I must agree with Astrid Faversham. The season has been an education. I hope for you also, Minerva!"

"You might call it that," said Minna. "But the season is not yet over."

She caught a glimpse of Oliver with Gabrielle, smiling down at her as they waltzed. She felt a fierce fire in her, flaming and burning.

She loved Oliver, and even if he did not return her love, she would save him from Gabrielle!

Chapter 12

MINNA TOSSED and turned that night, sleeping little. There must be some way to prevent that proposal the next day. Oliver must get to know Gabrielle better, and after that he would not dream of proposing.

But how to put it off? How to prevent them from riding out together?

She went down to breakfast early, she was the first one there. Percy was still asleep, said his valet, smiling. But for once Minna could not worry about her brother. She had more immediate problems on her mind.

François came down next, and something snapped in her mind. François looked weary and gloomy, and ate little. He was obviously as worried as she was.

When the footman had left the room, Minna said quickly, "François, I would talk with you."

"But of course, dear Minna."

"You love Gabrielle, don't you? Wouldn't you like to marry her?"

"Oh, these English," he murmured. "Sword blows at the breakfast table. Yes, I love her. Yes, I would marry her. But she has fallen in love with Oliver, I believe. Mr. Seymour seems a most worthy man—"

"Balderdash," said Minna vehemently. "She has no idea what Oliver is like at all! He would not suit her! She sees only his money, his jewels, his townhouse."

"Well, of course," said François, cutting his ham

178

methodically. "A Frenchwoman is usually very realistic. And he is most attracted to her."

"He is not!" stormed Minna, then had to stop as the footman reappeared with a fresh pot of hot water for the tea. She waited till he departed again.

"He was attracted to me," she said more quietly. "And he thinks she is—me! I mean, he would not like her character if he knew her. I mean—she is not his sort!"

François did not bother her with protestations and politenesses. He stirred his tea thoughtfully. "You are right," he said finally. "I think he is a good moral man. He would soon bore her, and then she would take lovers. It would not be a good marriage."

Minna gasped, but took up the suggestion. "I don't think so either. I think she would make you a good wife, because you understand her, and would not put up with nonsense, once you were married."

"You think not?" he asked, a little puzzled line on his sad, pleasant monkey face. "I am not so sure. She winds me around her fingers."

"That is the trouble," said Minna quickly, before anyone could interrupt them. "You must be firm with her! She admires firmness. She keeps testing you to see how far she can go. She always does, with all her beaux. When they weaken and give in to her, she is bored, and turns to someone new. She is searching for someone to—to tame her!" she added, with some help from a romantic Gothic novel she had been secretly reading.

"Tame her?" questioned François, looking interested. "You mean—like a wild horse?"

"Exactly! She needs someone who will hold the reins firmly and not let her get the bit in her teeth!"

"Ah."

"I am sure of it!"

"A firm hand."

"Yes, yes! She must be mastered. She must be told who is the master, and not allowed to run her own way! And François, I don't want her going with Oliver Seymour this morning!"

"If I tried to stop her, he would duel me," said François, with a sigh. "I am not a very good shot."

"Nonsense, it won't come to that. Listen, François, I have an idea!" She talked very rapidly now, to get the words in before someone came. Her mother always came down early.

"Tell your mother?" he suggested.

"No, she would become obstinate and find a way to meet him away from the house. No, I shall go instead!"

"She will not let you," he said, with a gleam of humor. "*She* would duel you, and her weapons are always sharp!"

"I know that from experience." She grimaced. "No, if I dress as Gabrielle—and go out with him in the carriage before anyone sees—and if you keep Gabrielle away—"

"Hum. I see. Yes!" he agreed. "But the question is—how? I cannot tie her to her bedpost!"

"Well, maybe not." Though the picture pleased. She began to think, turning over projects in her mind. Then her mother came in.

"Good morning, dear François, dear Minna. What a pleasant morning," said Mrs. Redmond, with a hopeful look in their direction.

The footman brought more tea as François rose to

seat Mrs. Redmond, and Minna said, "Good morning, Mother. Yes, a lovely day."

Mrs. Redmond poured her tea, said, "May I offer you another cup, François?"

"No," said Minna. "He is going to see the roses with me. Come along, François!"

He suavely concealed his surprise, and came with her. She marched him through the drawing room, out the French windows, to the rose beds.

"Most charming," he murmured.

"Not here, but to the back," she muttered, and put her hand in his arm to urge him faster.

He came with her, and surveyed the large summer-house with growing understanding.

"Ah," he said. "A pretty little gazebo in the town!"

"Yes, and the summerhouse has a lock on the door!"

"Ah, indeed!"

They went to examine the lock, the interior of the summerhouse. It was indeed a lovely little place, with white-painted benches, some flowery cushions on them, a pleasant breeze blowing through the lattice work, a view of the rose gardens. It was on the other side of the large house, away from the stables, out of view of the street. In short, a nice place to hide out. Minna showed him how the lock worked, for it was locked nights to keep out idlers who might wish to sleep there away from the streets and the law.

"But how will I get her here—when she has an appointment with Mr. Seymour?" mused François.

"It is simple—I hope," said Minna. "Oliver Seymour is very polite—and always early. If he should come early, I shall be outside ready to hop into his carriage, and not permit him to come in and speak to Mother.

181

And you keep Gabrielle here as long as you can—and pray—"

"I think I shall pray first, and get that out of the way," he said soberly. "When I have Gabrielle here, I shall need all my wits and tongue about me."

She did not even smile, she felt so anxious about their plan. "Yes, yes, however you will. I'll change her clock in the room, about fifteen minutes, and she will come down about quarter till eleven. You remind her of the right time, and ask her to come to speak to you here. Then—it is up to you—"

"Um. Well, I shall try. But do not blame me if it fails, and she accepts him! It may be that it is fate—"

"Nonsense! You must work for what you want, François! A strong man manages his own fates," she said with a frown at him. "Have courage, take what you want! Be sure of what you want, then take it! You love Gabrielle, don't you?"

"Yes, but I do not always like her," he said, meditatively. "However, life with her would be exciting, it has always been."

"I can imagine," she murmured. "Well, come back now, and tell Mother how much you like her roses, and she will give you more tea!"

François and Minna paused long enough at the flower beds to be able to comment on them, then returned to the house. Mrs. Redmond was in the hall, and gave Minna a very sharp look.

"Minna, you are quite red, why are you dashing about so rapidly this morning?"

"I want to wake Percy," said Minna quickly. "He has an appointment with Mr. Lavery this morning at ten."

182

As a red herring, it was a winner. Mrs. Redmond promptly forgot Minna.

"Good heavens, he is going to ask for—"

"Yes, I think so! It is wonderful, isn't it?"

"But I must go with him! I mean, it would be proper—and I must speak with Mrs. Lavery—dear me—dear Denise—are you quite sure, Minna?"

"Fairly sure," said Minna, not betraying confidences. "I do know Percy is to go there this morning—"

Percy's valet came through the hall. Mrs. Redmond stopped him. "Is my son up yet? Does he shave? What does he wear?"

"Yes, madam, yes, he shaves, and he wears the blue silk suit with the silver tie and his sapphires, madam." And the valet beamed, over the silver pot of shaving water.

"Go on, then, go on. Dear me, I must go with him. What shall I wear! Order the carriage for nine thirty, Minna, that's a dear." And she started up the steps.

"Wear your new lavender morning gown, Mother!" Minna called after her. "No gray or black today, if you will!"

"Of course, darling, the very thing." And Mrs. Redmond smiled happily down on her daughter. "Dear me, how happy I am, can it be true?—I must speak to Percy!"

"If you are making this up, all will be trouble for you, Miss Minna," said François idly.

"Making it up? Oh, no. They spoke to me last night," she blurted out. "But it will be perfect—Mother and Percy will be out calling on the Laverys while I—"

"While you get into more trouble." He sighed. "Dear me, I think you and Gabrielle are more alike than I had thought!" But he smiled down at her, and patted her shoulder kindly. "I shall prepare myself. Do you think I might have a bit more of the muffins?"

"Of course—do go in and sit down, François. I should not have dragged you away before you ate," she said, and sped up the stairs. How could he think of his stomach now?

She went through her wardrobe, muttering feverishly under her breath, then called Jessie. She had out the yellow silk gown with the brown Spanish braid, a fine cream bonnet she had just trimmed with artificial flowers and veiling, and French-heeled shoes of cream silk.

"What in the world is going on this morning, miss?" said Jessie, with the blunt curiosity of a long-time servant. She helped fasten up Minna, and began to brush her hair. "Your mother calling for her lavender gown, dashing in to see Mr. Percy with only his dressing gown on—"

"She is going with him to propose to Denise Lavery," interrupted Minna. "Of course, it is a secret yet, Jessie!" She knew Jessie adored being in on secrets before others knew. "You must not say a word until they return."

"And you're going with them—to help propose?" asked Jessie disapprovingly.

"No, no, I must be hostess here with Mother gone!" said Minna, improvising. "What is Gabrielle doing?"

"She called for her bright blue gown, her blue bonnet and matching parasol, she said she is going out riding this morning," said Jessie. "I'll have to go back and do her hair, you know that."

"Yes, do that, Jessie. I'll finish mine," said Minna,
184

with unexpected generosity, and Jessie looked at her suspiciously.

When the maid had left, Minna carefully brushed out her hair in the old Gabrielle style, though for her it was not so extreme as Gabrielle Dubois wore. She worked tenderly with the curls and tendrils, admired her image, mused and dreamed, until it was late. She had heard Percy and her mother departing excitedly at about nine thirty. Now to get Gabrielle taken care of by François. Courage, François, she muttered.

At ten forty-five, she stole down the front steps furtively, to the immense curiosity of the footman near the front doors. Things were going on indeedy, he said to himself. All this dashing about this morning, and now Miss Minna being sly.

His face showed nothing of his feelings. She peered out the window near the front door, then hesitated.

"Has Madame Dubois come down?"

"Yes, miss, she went out with Mr. Claudel, into the rose garden."

"Oh, good!"

That settled, she hovered, on one foot then another, until the footman's curiosity drove her into the drawing room. At the first sound of the carriage outside, she dashed to the door. It was Oliver, in a dashing black carriage with a hood and the two magnificent blacks.

"Open the door, quick!"

The footman did so, Minna held her breath, then went outdoors smiling.

"Good morning, Oliver!" She had almost forgotten her French accent. "How beautiful zis day is!"

"Good morning, Gabrielle!" He was about to hand the reins to the footman and get down.

"No, no, don't get down! The horses should not stand!"

Oliver gave her a long strange look. Minna or Gabrielle had never before presumed to advise him about his horses!

"They should not?" he inquired, too gently.

She knew her face was red as a beet. "And Mother is not home—I mean *Tante* Betsy—" she said, in a mutter she hoped he had not heard. "No one is home but me—and I am ready to go!"

"Most interesting," he said, and held out his hand. "Come up then. Yes, right here—that's it!"

She landed almost in his lap, and straightened herself with an effort. He clucked to the large handsome horses, and they set off.

"Well, well, what a glorious day!" he said merrily. "So you are ready to go, are you? And no one is home? Where has everyone gone?"

"Oh, dear, it is a secret," she said, in some confusion. But perhaps it would distract him. "I mean—well—all shall know soon."

"May I know soon?" He peered under her bonnet and smiled devastatingly at her. "How beautiful you are today—Gabrielle!"

"Thank you—very much! You see—Percy is proposing to Mother—I mean—and his mother is—I mean—Percy goes to Mr. Lavery to propose—"

He waited patiently until she got her tongue untwisted. He bowed and smiled to someone on the sidewalk, and she did also, without knowing in the least who was there.

"My cousin—Percy—hopes to marry Denise Lav-

186

ery," she finally told him slowly. "And his—mother—goes with him—"

"Ah. Splendid. So that little matter is straightened out," said Oliver. "And where is Minna?"

Ah, indeed. Where was Minna? Her mind sought frantically.

"Out with Monsieur Claudel," she said brightly.

"Really? I am shocked," he said sternly. "I don't believe he is fit company for a young girl!"

Oh, dear.

"But François is a darling man!" cried "Gabrielle" to her escort. "He is very sweet—very nice—"

"I am sure of it. I just explained that he was not fit company for Minna!" explained Oliver patiently. "I think we should go after them. Where did they go?"

Minna could have wept. "I have no idea," she said sullenly. "I thought we were going for a drive in the country?"

"You do not care what happens to your little innocent cousin?"

"Of course I care, very much. François does care also, I am sure, and will take every care of her!"

"I see. Thank you for your assurances."

He was silent, then, driving the carriage deftly through the London streets, avoiding a dray with inches to spare, avoiding a stagecoach and its merry passengers hanging from windows and the roof. Finally the traffic cleared, and he turned into a country road, away from the turmoil and bustle of the roads to and from London-town.

"Ah, this is better, much prettier. We are headed for a pretty country inn," he explained, smiling down at her. "I have bespoke a good nuncheon there, and we

187

can rest and drink some fine French wines, they have promised."

She drew a great breath of relief. That was much better. "I shall enjoy it immensely. It is a lovely day for May—"

"May is a pretty month. All the flowers," and with his whip he indicated the tangle of primroses on a country lane, a welter of bright Queen Anne's lace and chicory along the road.

"I don't care if they are weeds," she said happily. "I glory in the colors and shapes of them. Would it not be sad if all that was gone, and only gravel and sand lay there?"

"It would indeed." He seemed to relax, and began to hum as the horses clopped steadily along. They came in about another hour to a country inn, and he drove into the stable yard.

A big beaming landlord in an immense white apron came rolling out to greet them and help her down. Stableboys came also, to take the horses and wipe them down.

Oliver followed her into the inn, and they found a little room set aside for them. The crude wooden table in the center had been set with immaculate white cloths. And in the center were some yellow primroses like those along the lane.

Minna exclaimed over them. The landlord beamed. "Me datter picked 'em fer ye," he explained. "Said as gentry always likes them things."

He bustled out to order the food brought in. Minna removed her velvet cloak, Oliver set it aside. They sat down at the table, and he poured out some white wine for her that sparkled and bubbled.

188

It was delicious, though it tickled her nose. She wrinkled it. "Oh, what is this?" she said. "Can it be champagne? I only had it twice!"

"Yes, it is champagne," he said, and gave her that odd look again, that long thoughtful look. But he smiled, and teased her, "Do drink up! I know you will want more than that to satisfy your thirst!"

She knew better, wine went straight to her head. She shook her head, and set down the glass after a couple sips. Oliver drank his down, and poured more. The landlord brought in puff pastries and snails and a plate of pâté.

Minna had never never liked snails, no matter how prepared in melted butter nor broiled in juice, nor in puff pastries. Percy had put one down her neck when she was small, before he became more considerate a brother.

"I cannot eat these," she muttered, apologetically.

"But you told me last night you adored them!" he exclaimed. "I asked you especially!"

She was mortified, and terrified. So he and Gabrielle had discussed this! And what else?

"You are teasing me." He smiled. He put one to her lips. "Come ahead, eat it!"

She closed her eyes, and swallowed, shuddering. What must she do for love?

"There, is it not delicious?" he cried. "Come ahead, another one!"

"No, no, I will have pâté," she said, and reached quickly and rudely for that dish. She spread pâté on thick brown bread, and ate it eagerly. It was oyster pâté, her favorite. "Um, delicious."

"You are certainly changeable, Gabrielle!" he said,

189

smilingly, and sat down opposite her. "Only last night you told me you are deathly sick on oysters! What am I to think of you?"

Minna raised her gaze slowly, and began to study Oliver's brown, cheerful face. What made her feel so suspicious? What twinge made her fear him? Did he suspect she was not Gabrielle? Should she confess?

No, no, no, she wanted his proposal! She wanted him on his knees to her. She wanted to tell him how he had been mistaken in poor plain dowdy dull Minna! Then she would accept him! The game was almost played out, she could not call a halt now! Only one more hand, and it was done!

So she swallowed, answered somehow, drank more champagne, which made her feel very warm, and ate snails and pâté both.

The landlord returned with chicken, and she ate some of that, though her appetite seemed to have fled. Oliver plied her with champagne, she begged for a cup of tea.

"She is only teasing," Oliver told the landlord, shaking his head. "She is French, and detests tea, she told me so only last evening. Bring another bottle of champagne!"

Minna could have chopped off Gabrielle's head without resorting to a guillotine. She was parched. Oliver finally allowed the landlord to bring hot black coffee, which helped a little.

She could not eat a single almond pastry, and Oliver mourned aloud. Minna was certain by now there was a twinkle in his gray eyes.

Oliver leaned back and surveyed the girl opposite

him. Did he look more ominous now? She could not meet his gaze.

"Well, *Gabrielle*," he drawled. "We must drive on, it grows late. Almost five. Tell me, is there not something you wished to tell me?"

She stiffened. Had he guessed? What did he mean?

"I am sorry?" She faltered. "Tell you—what?"

"Isn't there something? You were going to tell me about your life—your lovers. You were going to confess that of all the men in your life, you had never loved a one before me. Wasn't that it?"

Minna stared. What had Gabrielle said last night? Her mind whirled in confusion. "L-lovers? But I have not—I mean—only my 'usband—my dear Gaspar—"

He gazed at her thoughtfully, and now he did look grim. "Come, we must depart, it grows dark soon," he said. He paid the landlord, and picked up Minna's cloak. He wrapped her in it, and hustled her out to the carriage waiting for them.

When he drove out of the inn yard, he turned into another road.

"This is not the road back to London," she said quickly. She pointed to a signpost. "See, there? London, eighteen—it is that way."

"I always prefer to take a road I have not taken before," he said oddly, and slapped the reins so briskly the blacks started into a brisk trot, fairly racing along the dusty country lane.

It was darker, much darker, she thought. She glanced at the sky. The sun had not set, but the trees were so thick she thought it was late under the trees. Very late. Dark. Ominous.

191

"I wish to return home," she said, her voice trembling.

"My dear Gabrielle! We have all the day!" he said, reassuringly, but his voice was cold. "You came quite willingly!"

"For a drive in the country," she said. "I have enjoyed it immensely! Th-thank you! But I should like—t-to go-go home now, p-please!"

"Not quite yet," he said, gazing straight ahead into the dim thicket of trees ahead. "Gabrielle, you have been a little tease! But the reckoning always comes! You have told me, and I have guessed, that you had many lovers. Do you not wish to add an English one to your list—before you return to your gay bright Paris?"

Minna could have fainted on the spot. "L-lovers. Oh, no," she moaned. "You do not mean—"

"I can promise you I shall be a very gentle lover," he said, but he did not sound gentle. "Before we return home, I mean to taste to the full the promise of your lips—and your supple silky body! I have held you in the waltz, and in an embrace—but there were too many clothes in our way, dearest Gabrielle! Tonight, nothing shall be between us, there shall be nothing to separate us!"

"No." Minna was quite sure of that. "No, no, no! You must turn back! Please—I beg you—do not tease me—"

"You beg me not to tease you, when you have teased me madly since the first meeting? You have flirted with your eyes, you have promised with your kisses. You cannot now deny me, Gabrielle!"

She wanted to scream, but there was no one to hear

192

but the mettlesome horses, the silent dark trees that skimmed the top of the carriage, the sky that brooded over them. The sun had disappeared behind a dark cloud. So had her hopes, her bright spirits, and the warmth from the champagne. She shivered violently from fear.

"You would not do this to me, Oliver," she quavered. "I beg you—for the friendship you bear to—to my dearest *tante—Tante* Betsy—and to M-Minna—"

Oliver easily transferred the reins from both hands to one, and slipped his free arm about her waist. He pulled her to him, quite crushing her bonnet against his shoulder. He took a quick glance at the quiet road, then bent to her face.

"I'll have a taste of what you'll be giving me soon," he said thickly. And his mouth came down hard on hers, pressing urgently. His tongue went into her open surprised mouth, almost choking her. "Ahhh—" he said.

"No," squeaked Minerva, when he raised up for a moment. "Oh, no, no, no—"

"Why not?" He breathed in her ear, and kissed the lobe.

"You'll fright—the horses!"

"You are right, we will wait until we get to the inn," he assured her, and took his arm from her waist, and gave his attention fully to the horses.

"What—inn?" she gasped, straightening her bonnet with shaking hands. "What—inn? We must get back to London!"

"Not tonight, my dear," he said.

Chapter 13

MINNA FELT quite petrified with fright. Surely Oliver Seymour, a nice gentleman who had always been rather kind, would not force a lady to have an affair with him? He would not, of course, he was just teasing her!

But then—her mind went running on—he did not believe Gabrielle Dubois was a lady! She was a very merry widow indeed, who had boasted of her lovers to him! Oh, how could she have done that? Minna fumed, but it did no good.

"Was that why—why you asked Gabrielle—asked me—to come riding today?" She faltered.

"What? Oh—our conversation last evening?" he asked smoothly. "Yes, it was most enlightening. I had enjoyed our flirtation so much, yet I could not quite believe you were so willing to take an English lover! When you assured me that you would—" He smiled down at her. "I sent a footman out at first light to make the arrangements!"

Her suspicions were growing rapidly. Surely Gabrielle had not been so foolish as to say anything of the sort. Oliver must be teasing her. He must know she was Minna—or did he? Could Gabrielle have boldly invited him—oh, no, it was impossible—

Yet she, Minna, was naive and unworldly. She would have found it difficult to believe that Gabrielle Dubois would have lovers while her husband was alive. That Gabrielle would have her lover bring her to England. That she would take her lover into her room in her aunt's home.

Yes, Minna was naive. She did not really know much about society, and the world outside her own sheltered one. Perhaps Oliver was that much smarter than she, that he had taken for granted that Gabrielle was a woman ripe for an affair, that a few jewels would be most welcome—

And Minna had blundered into the trap she had thought she was setting for Oliver! She shivered.

"Cold?" asked Oliver cheerfully. "The inn is not far! And soon you shall be tucked up in a cozy bed!" And he laughed.

Minna glanced about furtively. Could she jump from the carriage and run? But the countryside was not conducive to such behavior. The trees grew thickly, the ditches were deep beside the rutted dirt road, no houses were in sight, not a farmer nor a herdsman appeared. She would be in more danger if she left the carriage than if she remained.

No, she must wait for the inn, and appeal to the landlord. He would be a decent sort, with a family, and he would understand about a foolish girl wishing to be safely returned to London—

It was not far. Soon there was a widening in the dirt road, and the junction was a graveled road. Oliver turned the horses into the road, and in a short distance there was the large inn.

The inn was white-washed, with a slate roof, and slanting gables that made it rather attractive. But in the light of the setting sun, it looked also rather dark and unlit. "Is it—opened?" she quavered. "It does look—rather d-deserted!"

"It is, dearest," Oliver assured her. "I wanted a place that was rather deserted. We must be private, you know, and I would not want to cause gossip!"

"I am pleased at your thoughtfulness," said Minna bravely. "But would it not be better to return to London at once—and have no cause for gossip at all? It is kind of you to consider my reputation—"

"Not *your* reputation, darling!" he said, sounding surprised. "I did not think you had one to save! I thought you were notorious in France! Was that not why your stepson turned you out?"

She gulped, and could not answer, appalled. What in the world had Gabrielle been thinking, to talk so?

"No, no, I was thinking of my reputation," he said sweetly. "After all, I must marry one day, to someone respectable and have sons! No, it would not do to get too bad a reputation!"

"I could slap you!" cried Minna, without thinking, she was so enraged at his callousness. "You do not consider me at all, only yourself! That is just like a man!"

"Of course, my dear. But it is women like you who tempt us and draw us on. Come now, let me help you down!"

He had drawn into the stable yard, and several stablehands gawked up at her curiously. She bit her lips, and let Oliver help her down, at least his hands were not covered with barnyard filth. Her head high in the cream bonnet, she swept into the wooden door of the inn.

A tall young man came forward, wiping his hands

196

on the wet bar apron. He was surly, dark, scowling at them. "You're the gent what wants the room upstairs?" he asked.

His dark eyes went over them impersonally. Minna had opened her mouth to appeal to him, but closed it again. There were scars on his dark face, a sneer on his mouth as he glanced at her, and took in the fine yellow gown and high-heeled shoes.

"That'll be a guinea, in advance," he said, and caught the coin Oliver threw him. Then he retreated, pointing up the stairs. "At the top, on the right, sir. You wants any food or drink, just give a holler."

"Right," said Oliver. "My carriage is being unhitched. I'll pay more if you have them bait the horses and rub them down. We'll be leaving in the morning."

"Aye, sir." And he departed. Oliver's hand went under Minna's arm, and he led her to the stairs.

"Up you go, Gabrielle," he said cheerily.

There was nobody about at all, no nice maids, no plump innkeeper's wife, no guests, not even a drinker in the bar. Minna dug in her high-heels and refused to move.

"No, I won't go up there!" she said shrilly. "You cannot force me! Oliver, this joke has gone far enough!"

"Joke?" he asked, gazing down at her, with some surprise. His gray eyes were intent. "Why should it be a joke?"

"It has to be," she said forlornly. "You would never treat me so! It is wrong—I never said—I never asked for such treatment—I am no—no—s-slut—"

"Tut, tut, I never said you were! No, you are a very high-class female, Gabrielle," he said gently. His strong arm pushed unexpectedly, and she was forced up the

197

first stairs. "Now, do not be difficult! I know you want me as much as I desire you! And it should be very enjoyable for us both. I have some experience in affairs of this sort—"

"You should be ashamed to say it!" she told him spiritedly.

"Ashamed?" He seemed surprised, and pushed her up another couple steps, in spite of her hanging back. His arm about her waist was unexpectedly powerful. He half lifted her up another step. "Dear me, I should think you would be happy for my experience! I am no stupid boy, to hurt you, or make you uneasy! I hope to give you as pleasant an experience as I crave for myself! And if you are thinking about payment, I have brought a little locket along, with a diamond center, that will please you. You told me diamonds are your favorites!"

"They are not!" she cried, childishly. "I like—I like jade best! And sapphires!"

"Tut, tut, you are in a difficult mood today! My dearest Gabrielle, only a few more steps—" And he hauled her up the last steps, and into a little sitting room.

She looked about frantically. He had a strange light in his gray eyes—he smelled of drink—too much wine—and he really thought she was Gabrielle Dubois—an experienced lover—

He came toward her, and unfastened her bonnet. He tossed it on the table. "Come now," he coaxed. "Don't be difficult! I don't mind wooing, but a fight is another matter! Let's not spend the entire evening in a tussle!"

She did not feel the same way. She would fight him as long as her strength held out! And in her present frantic state of mind, that would be a long time! She
198

bit and scratched him, and gasped, "I'll fight you all night! Oliver, don't do this—I will not allow you—"

He clasped his arm about her, while he tried to keep off her clawing hands with the other. "Come on, Gabrielle! Don't be coy and difficult!"

"I'm not coy!" she cried, half in tears. "I won't do this—it is horrible—let me go—I pray you—let me go—"

He looked down in her face, his arm slackened. His voice changed to a more gentle tone. "What is it, Gabrielle? Have I alarmed you by my demands? I will be a careful lover, if you do not madden me! Don't you realize that you have teased and tempted me quite long enough? From the very first evening, you have drawn me on to woo you. Why draw back now? What is wrong?"

There was an odd urgency in his tone. But Minna was more aware of the bedroom door opened behind her. And there was a bed in there, a wide bed with fresh sheets on it, all open and ready!

She glanced at the door to the rooms. Oliver had closed it, the bolt was drawn. It would take a couple minutes to open that, and meantime he would pounce.

"You are hurting me," she complained, standing very still in his arm. "Your hand on my wrist—"

"But you will scratch me with your kitten-claws if I let you go!" He laughed. Nevertheless, he released her wrist.

She wrenched herself from him in an instant, and fled to the bedroom. She slammed the door in his face, and groped for the bolt. Yes, it was there, a nice solid bolt. She slammed it home into the catch, and slumped against the door.

"Gabrielle!" He was there, right beyond the door. He was laughing. "Come on, darling, don't be so difficult! Open the door, and let me in. I don't want you alone— in our bedroom!"

She swallowed, and looked about the little room. Most of the space was taken up with the huge bed. But there was a small chest of drawers, a table with a pitcher of water and a basin, a couple of towels—no more. No poker, no fire, no weapon.

She had only a bolt between him and her. Nothing but a bolted door between herself and disgrace. Oh, he would soon know he had made a terrible mistake, that she was a virgin! But it would be much too late by that time!

He was drunken, he must be drunken, to do this to her!

But he had planned it! She recalled that now. He had sent out a footman, and had planned it all! It was deliberate!

She put her hand to her breast. He was laughing. Her heart thumped and thumped, and it made her out of breath.

"Come on, darling, open the door!"

She would not answer.

"Gabrielle!"

She tiptoed over to the window. The floor creaked. He went silent, she thought he listened at the door.

Cautiously, she peered from the square window. It was low slung, fastened with only a small latch. She twisted the latch, it opened. She peered from the window, found it was just above a slanting roof of slate. This must be one of the gables of the building. Outside was the stable yard. She could see the carriage in the

200

yard, and a stablehand was wiping down one of the black stallions.

Did she dare?

As a child she had been something of a tomboy. She had climbed trees with Percy, she had slid down roofs, she had even ridden horses bareback. But not for years!

"Gabrielle!"

She started nervously, listened.

"I have ordered some tea! Come out and have some!"

She swallowed. She was parched!

"Gabrielle! We can talk for a time if you wish. Talk honestly and frankly!"

Was there pleading in his voice? She hesitated.

His voice lowered, he was laughing again. "And bed can come later, when we wish it!"

Her mouth compressed. Frantically she looked about. Was there no woman about, no kind country woman who would understand and defend her, and give Oliver Seymour the scolding he deserved?

No woman about. Only the uncouth men in the stable yard, staring up at her in the window.

She withdrew, and sat down on the bed. It creaked. She winced.

"Have you gone to sleep in there, Gabrielle? Come out and have some tea? Um, it is good, so hot and full of milk!"

How could she think she loved him? He was crude, a bully, a vulgar conniving seducer of women!

Silence for a time, she brushed back her hair. She was hot and distracted and upset. The window was growing dark rapidly. The sun had gone down, a cock crowed sleepily, some birds gave hushed calls to each

201

other. A peaceful country scene—but for herself and Oliver!

The door rattled, she shot to her feet. She stared at the door, was the latch moving?

"Come on, Gabrielle! Unlock the door! If you don't, I'll break it down!" And a strong shoulder pushed at the door. It shuddered, but held.

But for how long?

"Gabrielle!"

"I'm thinking!" she cried, in a panic.

"Well, stop thinking and come out. You are wasting our night together!"

"Oliver, you have it wrong. I am not—not—"

"Not what, darling?" he asked eagerly.

"Not a loose female!" she called.

"Anything else?"

She was silent. So was he. She glanced about again. Not a weapon, nowhere. Not a block of wood, even.

It was pitch dark. She shivered. He would not be patient much longer. She heard him moving about, the clink of a cup and saucer. Oh, he was cruel!

Cautiously, she drew up the small table to the window and mounted it. She teetered on her French heels, got hold of the window ledge, and climbed up. Her dress caught, she gave it a tug. She tugged it harder, and it finally gave way with a soft rip of silk. Damn, her new yellow gown!

"Gabrielle!" The door shuddered again with the impact of his body against it. In a panic she climbed over the sill and onto the slate roof.

It was slippery, she tried to hold on, but there was little to hold. She slid and skidded down the sloping slate roof to the edge. With a little shriek she went over the edge, and landed on her backside in the dust of the stable yard.

She sat there. Nobody came. The boys must be inside, having their supper. She finally got up, brushed herself off, and ran!

She ran across the stable yard, avoiding the yellow glare of torches from the open inn back door. She ran into the field to the side of the inn, and panted as she rested against a massive oak tree.

She peered back at the inn. No sign of opening doors, no calls or yells. If the horses had been hitched up to the carriage, she would have tried to drive them back to London. But she could not hitch them up.

Ride bareback? Not those nervous sensitive black stallions! They would pitch her right off.

There was no help for it. She must walk back to London, and hope to get a stagecoach or a farmer's wagon in which to ride.

Her feet hurt. The French heels were not made for walking. She lifted her trailing skirts, and set out anyway; this would be better than seduction!

She walked into the fields, searching for the dirt road. Surely she had not missed it. The road must be right here—where was it?

She heard voices! A grumbling male voice!

Panicky, she stood still, did not move. But the gleam of her yellow dress in the darkness betrayed her. The two men had come out of the wheat field, and stared at her.

"By the devil—it's a female!" They came closer. She stared, wide-eyed, backing up slowly.

"A purty one!"

"It's our lucky night!" One man stepped up close to her and suddenly he reached out and grabbed.

Minerva screamed! She screamed piercingly. She had been so afraid, and now this man had her by the wrist—and it hurt—and he was grinning—his face so dirty she could scarce see any feature.

"Oliver—Oliver!" She screamed, without knowing she named him. "Oliver—help—help—help!"

Oliver had been more and more uneasy in the room. It was too quiet in the bedroom. Had Minna-Gabrielle fallen asleep? He had meant to have it out with her, and get her back to London in good time. But that girl was so stubborn!

"Gabrielle?" he called.

He heard nothing. No screech of bedsprings, no sobs. Nothing. No movement.

Uneasily he stood close to the door again. It was pitch dark outside. Damn the girl. Why did she have to be such a little idiot! He only meant for her to give in and admit what she had done!

"Gabrielle! I shall knock the door in!"

No sound.

"Minna!" he said at last. "Damn it, I know you are Minna. Open this door, and let us talk!"

No sound. Alarmed, he pushed at the door. It shuddered. He finally picked up a poker from the fire and smashed at the door where the latch was.

Two smashes, three, and the latch gave way. The door yawned open. He went inside, prepared to find tears, defiance, even a fight.

But the small room revealed nobody. No pretty little defiant redhead in a yellow gown. Nobody at all. The window swung open. The table stood beneath it.

He went over to the window, bewildered. He put his hands on the frame, and peered out. A fragment of cloth touched his fingers. He looked down at it, picked it from the broken nail. A piece of yellow silk!

"Minna!" he yelled out the window.

A stablehand came below, gazing up, holding a torch.

"Hey, mister, what's it?"

"A girl—did you see a girl—a lady in a yellow gown?"

"Yup! When you come in, mister!"

"I mean, just now!"

"Nope!"

Cursing under his breath, Oliver turned and ran out the door, and down the stairs. The landlord came from the taproom to stare.

"She's gone," said Oliver briefly. "Get me a couple of your men—we must search—"

He ran outdoors, the landlord following. The landlord was speaking to a couple of his stablehands, when they heard the scream, faintly on the night air.

"Oliver—Oliver—help!"

They all ran in the direction of the sound. Oliver heard the coarse laughter, and his blood ran cold.

The landlord sent a bellow before him. "Hey—hey—there she is—you let that lady be!"

The stablehands willingly added their halloos and bellows. Minna screamed again, and Oliver found her in a patch of grass, sitting in a billow of yellow silk. The men had taken to their heels.

"Oh, Oliver," wept Minna, tears streaming down her cheeks. He picked her up and hugged her to him.

"You foolish little Minna!" he said tenderly. "God, I could beat you."

"Best to beat them," said the landlord in his growl. He yelled to the hands to come back. "Let them be," he yelled. "They'll be armed."

The men came back, and accompanied them to the stable yard.

"Hitch up my horses, we'll go back to London," said Oliver wearily. "Oh, and fetch the lady's bonnet and my gear, if you will."

The landlord nodded, without a word, and clumped away. The hands brought out the black horses, and hitched up the carriage. Minna was weeping quietly, and steadily.

Lord, he had botched it badly!

She could have been killed!

As it was, she had had a terrible scare, and not just from the villains in the field. From himself! To be so terrified, she had run away from him, out the window and gone!

The carriage was put to, the landlord came back with Minna's bonnet, Oliver's coat and gloves and cane. Oliver paid him heavily, thanked the men, and they were off, to return to London.

Minna was controlling her tears, she was wiping her eyes with his handkerchief, and sniffing a bit, that was all. Oliver was thinking, as the horses paced steadily along the country road.

It could not go on like that. He could not endure it! No, it must be settled and done.

Minna had to give in! But tonight she was too tired and upset to think straight.

She was slumped beside him; the carriage seat was not all that comfortable for a tired lass.

"Lean against me," he said gruffly. "You're so

206

weary." He could not keep the tenderness from creeping in, though he meant to be strict with her.

"No, thank you," she said.

"God-a-mercy! Will you do as I tell you!" he roared.

She jumped, and then timidly leaned against his shoulder.

It was a long journey. Finally the lights of London that had gleamed in a distance began to get brighter and more clear. As they came closer, he kept a watch for footpads on foot or thieves in carriages. It was close to midnight.

They turned into the main London road, and clip-clopped along. The horses were tired, so was he. It had been a long, sobering day.

And finally they turned into the street where the Redmonds lived. And he saw the torches at the gate, the footman keeping watch, and every light in the house ablaze. The Redmonds were waiting up for them.

The footman was there, the door opened as he drew up. Another footman came out, one of the older ones, to help Minna down.

"Miss Minna—God be thanked," he breathed, as his strong hands lifted her bodily from the carriage. He ventured to glare up to Oliver. "Mr. Seymour, sir, we been a-worrying!"

"I'll come in for a bit," he said drily. "Will you take care of the horses? They are too tired to give trouble."

The younger footman took the reins, and Minna led the way into the house. Her mother was just inside in the hallway, and Oliver braced himself to meet her reproaches.

Chapter 14

WHEN MINNA SAW her mother's weary wrinkled face, tears came to her eyes.

"Oh, Minna, where have you been?" asked Mrs. Redmond, and held out her arms.

Minna half fell into them. Her mother led her gently into the drawing room. Percy was there, and Gabrielle, and François Claudel, and the maids, and—

Oh, it was all too much. She could not tell her mother in front of all of them.

Oliver had followed her in. "It was my fault, Mrs. Redmond," he said gravely.

"No, it was mine," confessed Minna, in a subdued tone. She pulled the bonnet strings, and dragged her bonnet from her aching head. "Oliver, I am so sorry. But I have deceived you. I—I masqueraded as my cousin—Gabrielle Dubois. I am Minerva Redmond."

He was gazing down at her, the oddest look on his handsome face. Regret, laughter, sympathy—she could not decipher it all.

"But where have you been?" insisted her mother. "Gabrielle said Oliver invited her for a ride in the country. But she was conversing with Francois, and forgot the time—"

Minna could not help giving her cousin an involuntary guilty glance. But Gabrielle leaned back in the cushions languidly, and said nothing, watching all alertly with her narrowed green eyes.

"Yes, yes. But I went with Oliver—I mean—he thought I was Gabrielle—" Desperately she turned to Oliver, her eyes lowered, so she could not read the growing contempt he must feel. "I must tell you—I have pretended to b-be—G-Gabrielle—for these weeks—she arrived only a few days ago—to h-help me out of the c-coil—"

"I sent for Gabrielle," said Betsy Redmond, with a sigh. "I could see no other way out of this. Minna pretending to be her cousin—flirtations going on—I should never have permitted it, Mr. Seymour. It was quite dreadful!"

"I was wrong," said Minna, miserable, ready to cry again. "I apologize to—to everyone—for the t-trouble I have c-caused—"

"But where have you been, all night?" demanded Percy, coming up to Oliver. "You took my sister out in the country—and it is quite past midnight! What of her reputation? This not like you, Seymour!"

"One might say—I was maddened," said Oliver thoughtfully. "However, I mean to make amends. Minerva, I have the honor and distinct pleasure to ask you to marry me. I will cherish you, respect you, welcome you into my family, as I am sure my mother and sister will do. Will you marry me?"

The air in the drawing room seemed to warm. After a hushed silence, Percy said, "Well, I did not know you meant—of course, Minna will have you, I am sure!"

"I would rather hear it from her, if you will," said Oliver gently. "Well, Minna? Will you have me?"

He took her hand, her cold little paw, so dusty and

dirty, her gloves gone. She swallowed, unable to meet his gaze. He would feel such contempt for her! This was all he could do, he had disgraced her—her reputation—and it was all her fault— Such confused thoughts went through her mind, she could not speak.

Mrs. Redmond nudged her daughter. "Minna? Will you? I quite approve—if this is what you want!"

Minna finally managed to nod, and said hoarsely, "I—yes—I will—if he wants—"

Oliver seemed to relax a trifle, he squeezed her hand and bent to kiss her cheek. This was not the way she had meant it to happen. She could have wept again. She had wanted him on his knees before her, humiliated, burning with love for her—and Minna haughty in her best jade silk—condescending—

"Well, that is fine then!" said Percy heartily, with relief. "Congratulations to you both! Denise and I are engaged, you know! Shall you beat us to the altar? We mean to marry in June!"

"June is a good time," said Oliver. "Perhaps we might make it a double ceremony!"

"Oh, excellent idea," said Percy. "Saves all kinds of trouble! Just one reception!"

His mother intervened hastily. "I am sure it is not necessary to decide all this tonight, it is rather late! Mr. Seymour, my good wishes to your mother, we will speak later this week concerning this! I asure you I am most pleased with the happy event. Minna seems very tired, I will put her to bed!" she added sternly.

"Yes, yes, excellent idea. Minna, may I call upon you tomorrow morning?"

She nodded, still feeling so humiliated she could not

raise her look to his face. "Yes—perhaps at eleven," she said dully.

"Fine, I shall come." He gave her hand a final squeeze, and dropped it to her side.

"Well, if I may say—" said Gabrielle, rising languidly. "All this day has been most exciting. François and I are engaged also! Yes, he has swept me off my feet!" she said, drily.

"Indeed!" Mrs. Redmond turned to her niece in surprise. "You—Gabrielle—and Mr. Claudel? Well, I am not amazed, but I am so pleased. I believe you are quite suited, and he has—proved his devotion to you," she added.

"Yes—he has, hasn't he?" said Gabrielle, with a smile, reaching out her hand grandly to François. He took it, kissed it gallantly, as Minna watched in some envy. Now, that was the way to carry off an announcement! She could not blame Oliver for not kissing her dirty hand; trust Gabrielle to have clean hands with jewels on them, and perfume, all ready for such an occasion.

"You have made me the most happy man in the world," said François Claudel, with emotion. He straightened, and his sad monkey face seemed more sad.

"We shall marry in France, however," said Gabrielle. "Among our friends there. I fear we must depart soon, dear Tante Betsy. You have been so ver' kind to us! However, we must depart ver' soon!"

Mrs. Redmond hid her relief admirably. "Must you? But first you must celebrate with us, that Percy and also Minna are engaged!"

"Lord, what parties," muttered Percy, as though he

211

had just been shocked into awareness of the many festive occasions before him, before he could return to his beloved estates.

Oliver gave Percy, and then Gabrielle and François his most sincere congratulations on the happy occasion, and then made his departure. He did not kiss Minna again.

The door closed after him, the carriage clopped away. Minna drooped.

"Well," said Gabrielle. "You are a sly one, Minna! I could not conceive what had happened when I was locked into the summerhouse with François! Then I understood that you were so ver' jealous of me!"

Minna raised her weary head. "He is in love with me," she said clearly. "I could not let you get away with anything, Gabrielle! He is not suited to you!"

Gabrielle shrugged daintily. "Perhaps not, he is very dull," she conceded. "François understands me best of all!"

Behind her back, François winked solemnly at Minna, and her spirits rose a little. At least she had managed that a-right!

Then Minna went to bed. Mercifully, her mother did not remain to question her on the day's activities. Jessie did give her a scold, though, as she helped her into her nightrail.

"Keeping the household up to all hours!" she said, tending to her charge as though she were a small girl. "I'll do the buttons, miss! And away all the day, alone, with a gentleman! You know better than that, Miss Sly!"

"Yes, I know better. It wasn't what I had—hoped," sighed Minna. "Oh, well, it all turned out—didn't it?"

"He'll do the honorable," conceded Jessie, bluntly. "He's a gent, that is sure. Couldn't get a nicer feller. We was talking below stairs, all of us, and said as how you couldn't ask for a nicer gentleman, always polite and thoughtful to anybody, no matter what his station. Yes, you could do a lot worse, Minerva Redmond!"

Minerva thought so too, sighing and tossing on her bed that night. She had taken advantage of his kindness, and if she had an ounce of generosity in her, she would break the engagement and let him go!

Oliver had proposed to her only because he had compromised her by taking her off alone, and not returning until midnight. He was doing the only honorable thing to clear her reputation, for few would talk when the outing was promptly followed by an announcement of their engagement.

Yet Oliver could not be happy about this! He could not be. And he had not seemed happy tonight at all.

Oh, what a tangled coil she had brought about when she had impulsively decided to masquerade as a French jade! She remembered how Oliver had said he meant to acquire some French jade, and tears rolled down her cheeks.

She had brought herself down with a crash, and Oliver with her! She had not meant to do that, she vowed. She had only wanted to avenge herself for the cruel words he had spoken lightly, she was sure, to that hateful Astrid Faversham.

Oliver had tried to apologize. She should have accepted that graciously, and let the incident pass. That was what a true lady would have done!

But no, Minna had had to have her impulsive way! She had defied her mother and gone ahead in this crazy

213

masquerade, and look what trouble she had brought on them all! And mostly onto Oliver!

She felt he did not want to marry her. He was older, mature, serious, a man of the world. Why should he marry a flighty silly chit like Minna? Oh, he was probably already regretting his proposal! Yet he was so honorable, he would force himself to go through with it!

The only thing she could do, the only moral thing to do, was to confess all to him, and break the brief engagement. She had to let him go. She would not tie him to a life of misery with a woman he did not love. It was too great a sacrifice for him.

Oddly enough, when Minna had reached this conclusion, she was able to go to sleep. She was satisfied, she had come to the right decision. She must do what was right for all, especially for Oliver.

Her reputation would suffer for a time, but she was sorry, and her mother would forgive her.

Her penalty would be a lifetime of living without Oliver. And that was terrible, she thought, as she wakened the next morning. A lifetime without Oliver! Never to see him close again, never to feel his kisses on her cheeks, on her mouth. Never to have his arms about her, his fierce embrace that brought her body so closely to his that she felt she melted against him!

It was a very subdued girl that Jessie saw that morning. The maid gave her a keen look.

"What will ye wear this morning, with your beau coming to visit you, Miss Minerva?"

"The blue muslin," she said sadly.

Jessie started to protest, then compressed her lips, shook her head, and got out the little blue muslin. It
214

had not been worn recently, and the ironing girl had it bright and fresh.

Minerva donned it, and sat silently to have her hair brushed. Jessie must have sensed her mood, for she brushed the hair demurely, not in the old tight coronet, but in a close wave that just outlined Minna's small, shapely head.

"No muslin bonnet, I cannot endure it," said Minna, and Jessie agreed.

"Nay, you're no spinster, Minna," she agreed cheerfully, dropping her formality. "There now, you look a good sight. Not like that French hussy, but a sight prettier, just as ye are!"

Minna went down to breakfast, and had the pleasure of Percy and his quiet happiness. Percy had much to say about his fiancée, how pretty was Denise, what a good girl, what a sensible girl, what a fine wife she would make, how happy he was. Minna agreed with him about it all.

He was off to take Denise to the lending library that morning. Minna thought the books would not take much of their attention. How well suited they were. She would be so happy to welcome Denise as her sister. And Mary, Amelia, and young Jane were all so charming, it would be pleasant to have them visit this summer.

Mrs. Redmond came down, yawning, as Percy departed. She came in to breakfast, and her eyes sharpened as she saw Minna in blue muslin.

She sat down, and poured out tea. "So Oliver Seymour comes this morning," she said. "You'll not be foolish, Minna?"

"No, Mother," said Minna dully. She waited till the

215

footman left the room before adding quietly, "I cannot marry him. Oliver asked me only—only because of the fix—that I pushed him into. It would not be fair—"

"Oh, dear, I was afraid of that," said her mother simply. "Are you quite sure he has no tenderness for you, darling?"

"Oh, I think he has tenderness," said Minna bitterly. "But not—not love!"

"Well." Betsy sipped thoughtfully. "Do give him a chance to say so, though, darling," she urged. "I could wish you were not quite so quick of tongue! Let him speak!"

Minna promised, then went to the drawing room to wait. She heard François's voice later, but not Gabrielle. She could not endure to speak to Gabrielle this morning.

No one came into the room. She was grateful for that. She sat quietly, composing her thoughts. About ten until eleven, she heard a carriage drive up. Oliver Seymour, on time as usual. She clenched her fists. She must be strong! But not quick of tongue!

Oliver came into the room and shut the door after him. He came over to her. "Good morning, my darling," he smiled, and before she knew what he was about to do, he drew her up and into his arms. She was drawn to his warm body, and he bent his head.

She caught her breath, her mouth opened to protest. They had much to discuss! Oliver put his mouth on hers, and his lips clung warmly. Oh, it was so sweet, so dear, so exciting!

Minna answered his kisses just as warmly, her hands clinging to his arms. He lifted his head finally and smiled down at her.

"There. That was what I wanted," he said, with satisfaction.

"Oh, Oliver," she said. "I had not meant to do that. I was going—I must say—"

"Before you speak, let me say what I came to say." He interrupted swiftly, and she thought there was something odd in his expression. "Pray, sit down, Minna." And gently he pushed her down once more onto the sofa.

"What?" she quavered. "W-what do you—wish—"

To her amazement, Oliver sank onto his blue silk-clad knee as gracefully as a courtier. He put one white-gloved hand to his breast, and fixed his gaze on hers earnestly.

"Minerva," he said solemnly. "I have long admired you, and your fine family. I knew you were a fine and excellent child, a lovely young girl. When you grew to maturity, I noted with pleasure your intelligence, your kindness, your gentleness."

Was she dreaming? Could it be true? Or was he mocking her? She stared at him, with wide green eyes, scarcely breathing.

"It distressed me to see you remain shy, long after you should have grown more confident of your charms and worth. The night that I mocked you, I was but teasing, hoping to waken you to how—how silly it was that you should dress as a child, as a dowd. Minna, I swear to you I never meant to hurt you."

"Oh—" She swallowed, and found her voice. "It did—not matter—really—Oliver—"

"It did matter. I was wrong, I was foolish. But I am sure it was fate that caused this to happen. When you were driven by fury to play your masquerade, the gods

217

must have been laughing kindly at us, Minerva! For it was then I grew to understand that I loved you."

"Oh—" she breathed, enraptured. How beautifully he talked!

"I was fooled for a time, I admit. But behind the brazen flirtation, the bold costumes, I sensed a tender, gentle spirit, a generous sweet passion. And so did I fall more deeply in love with you, Minna!"

She could not speak. He paused, anxiously, then went on slowly.

"And when I proposed last night, Minna, I sensed that you were troubled, as I was. I had not meant it to happen like that. I truly frightened you yesterday, in my attempts to make you confess what you had done. I am so sorry for that. I do swear it shall never happen again! If you but bring yourself to trust me, I shall protect you rather than harm you, keep you from danger rather than thrust you into danger, love you and cherish you all our days—"

"Oh, yes, Oliver," she whispered.

"Yes?"

"Yes, I love you," she said, with a radiant smile. She put her hands on his outstretched hands, and allowed him to draw her up once more, and into his embrace.

His mouth covered hers, with passion and gentleness. She put her arms about his neck, and clung. His body was so strong and fine, she could lean against him with confidence. His hands were so gentle, she would put her heart into them and never regret. She nestled against him, and felt his lips brush her forehead.

"And what were you going to tell me, darling?" he murmured.

Minna stiffened. Oh, what she had almost said!

218

But there must be no more deceit between them.

She lifted her head and looked up into his clear gray eyes. "I was going to say—I could not marry you, Oliver, without love," she said softly. "I love you so much, and it would not be right to make you—I mean—you proposed because you had—compromised me—and it was not right—your sacrifice—"

His eyes softened, he smiled down at her, and bent to brush his lips against her cheek.

"Brave girl," he said. "Now you are honest with me! Do you love me, then?"

"Oh, yes, I love you dearly!"

She was kissed for her confession, and time slid away for a bit. They finally came back to reality, and sat together on the sofa, hands clasped, smiles mingling, eyes ready to gaze with confidence. He reached into his pocket and drew out a little ring box of green jade, and opened it. He showed her the ring inside, of a huge diamond surrounded by five fine emeralds of green fire.

"Like your eyes, my darling," he said tenderly. He slipped it onto her finger. "I have also some jade jewelry for you," he teased. "But that is only a bracelet and pendant, some earbobs, and such. I know you prefer jade!"

"I shall love it," she said, with a mischievous smile, her spirits rebounding rapidly. "It shall remind me of how I played the jade for you—and you did not despise me, Oliver!"

"Nay, rather I adored you the more!" He laughed. "What a tease you were! When I came to realize you were not a French jade, a wicked widow, the Madame Dubois, and were Minna, my Minerva—what a shock it was! You had changed before my eyes!"

"And are you disappointed," she asked, half wistfully, leaning against his breast. "Are you disappointed, that I am only Minna? Plain, demure Minna?"

"But you are not," he assured her. "I am happy to marry my spirited and beautiful bride. You were always lovely. However, in your masquerade, you did change and come out of your shell, darling. I had always admired you. You were smart, good, kind. But—" And he smiled teasingly.

"What?" she demanded eagerly, hungry for his praises.

He kissed her forehead. "When you masqueraded as your cousin, and acted a part, you did not so much become like that Frenchwoman! You became what you had the potential of becoming, a bright and wonderful woman. I observed you with pleasure. Many beautiful women are cold and selfish, they are so charmed with themselves!"

"Some—can be," she agreed demurely.

"But, darling, you were not. I watched and listened as you moved among our friends. And you were kindness and thoughtfulness themselves, to the other shy ones. You showed your generous helpful nature to others. I was—most pleased with you, I must admit! And amazed!"

"Surprised?" she asked, not quite so pleased. "Did you think me selfish? I suppose I have been—to Mother and Percy—thinking of myself first."

"No, no! Rather, you forwarded Percy's courtship very cleverly, and I must say he found himself a fine wife! I shall enjoy having Percy and Denise as my in-laws! And never did you distress nor disgrace your lady mother! Rather you showed her good training of you,
220

and her example! Even in playing a jade, you did not forget you were a lady!"

"Oh, Oliver, you say kind things," she whispered. "I fear I was brazen, a flirt, with you."

He smiled a bit, and whispered in her ear, "Not more than I enjoyed!" he said. And he bit the lobe.

She sighed. "And when we—marry," she said shyly. "Will you—continue to—I mean—treat me—I mean—"

"I shall always treat my wife as the lady she is," he avowed solemnly. "In public, she shall be honored!"

"Oh—thank you, Oliver," she murmured, a bit disappointed.

"Of course—in our bedroom," he added, into her ear, with a rumble of passion in his deep voice. "In our bedroom—I shall treat you as my very own French jade!"

And he kissed her fiercely.

CURRENT CREST BESTSELLERS

☐ THE MASK OF THE ENCHANTRESS   24418 $3.25
   by Victoria Holt
   Suewellyn knew she wanted to possess the Mateland family castle,
   but having been illegitimate and cloistered as a young woman, only
   a perilous deception could possibly make her dream come true.

☐ THE HIDDEN TARGET   24443 $3.50
   by Helen MacInnes
   A beautiful young woman on a European tour meets a handsome
   American army major. All is not simple romance however when she
   finds that her tour leaders are active terrorists and her young army
   major is the chief of NATO's antiterrorist section.

☐ BORN WITH THE CENTURY   24295 $3.50
   by William Kinsolving
   A gripping chronicle of a man who creates an empire for his family,
   and how they engineer its destruction.

☐ SINS OF THE FATHERS   24417 $3.95
   by Susan Howatch
   The tale of a family divided from generation to generation by great
   wealth and the consequences of a terrible secret.

☐ THE NINJA   24367 $3.50
   by Eric Van Lustbader
   They were merciless assassins, skilled in the ways of love and the
   deadliest of martial arts. An exotic thriller spanning postwar Japan
   and present-day New York.

Buy them at your local bookstore or use this handy coupon for ordering.

COLUMBIA BOOK SERVICE, CBS Inc.
32275 Mally Road, P.O. Box FB, Madison Heights, MI 48071

Please send me the books I have checked above. Orders for less than 5 books
must include 75¢ for the first book and 25¢ for each additional book to cover
postage and handling. Orders for 5 books or more postage is FREE. Send check
or money order only. Allow 3-4 weeks for delivery.

Cost $_____ Name_____

Sales tax*_____ Address_____

Postage _____ City_____

Total $_____ State_____ Zip_____

*The government requires us to collect sales tax in all states except AK, DE,
MT, NH and OR.

Prices and availability subject to change without notice.   **8229**